THE END OF
FOREVER

Also from Steve Berry

Also from M.J. Rose

M.J. Rose and Steve Berry

M.J. Rose and C. W. Gortner

THE END OF FOREVER

A CASSIOPEIA VITT ADVENTURE

By M.J. Rose
and Steve Berry

BLUE
BOX
PRESS

The End of Forever
A Cassiopeia Vitt Adventure
By Steve Berry and M.J. Rose

Copyright 2021 Steve Berry and M.J. Rose
ISBN: 978-1-952457-52-4

Published by Blue Box Press, an imprint of Evil Eye Concepts, Incorporated

If you prick us, do we not bleed?
If you tickle us, do we not laugh?
If you poison us, do we not die?
And if you wrong us, shall we not revenge?

William Shakespeare

Chapter One

SUNDAY

CASSIOPEIA VITT HATED FUNERALS.

It was a sentiment that she and Cotton Malone shared. One of many. Which made them perfect for one another. She wished he was here, but he'd been unable to make the journey from Denmark to northern Spain.

She stood in the harsh July sun. Over a hundred white lilies draped the coffin, and over a thousand tears were being shed. Esmerelda Fortuna had been a lawyer of great renown. Sixty-seven at the time of her death, she lived an extraordinary life dedicated to helping others. Many of those crowded around the gravesite had been clients, many more friends, some family. They'd all come to say goodbye to the strongest woman Cassiopeia had ever known. Aunt Esmerelda, as she'd called her since childhood, though they were not related by blood. Instead, Esmerelda had been her family's lawyer, the one her father had turned to time and again for help, even after his death.

She tried to imagine a life without her.

Her own parents had died almost twenty years ago. Afterward, Esmerelda became mother, friend, and confidant in addition to handling the Vitt family trust. Esmerelda's daughter, Jocasta, who now stood beside her in the sun, was Cassiopeia's best friend. They held hands, Jocasta's grip tight, moist, and unrelenting. From beneath sunglasses, tracks of tears rolled down her dear friend's cheeks.

Which made her wonder.

Why had she not cried?

Easy. Crying was tough for her. Emotions were better kept inside, under lock and key, brought out only when absolutely necessary. Surely she would cry before the day was out, but that would be back at her hotel, with the door closed and no one else around. Her family's former ancestral home stood nearby, but she'd sold the estate a few months back after dealing, thanks to Esmeralda's help, with one last family legacy. She'd laid those ghosts to rest thinking all was right with the world.

Then this.

She and Jocasta both wore black dresses, black hats, and black shoes. Jocasta's hair was rolled in a neat twist. Her own long raven locks were held back with barrettes. Esmerelda would have demanded nothing less than a high level of style and elegance. *Appearances matter,* she'd said many times. All part of that all-important first impression, *a narrative that is totally within your control, so work it to your advantage.*

More truths from a smart lady.

Pedro Fortuna, Jocasta's brother, stood next to them. He was a gemologist who divided his time between Brazil and London. Of late, brother and sister had been estranged, but when they were younger all three of them had been inseparable. Both Pedro and Jocasta had always been a fixture in the Vitt home. She'd sailed with them many times on her parents' boat. They'd vacationed together. Attended the same schools. And then they'd gone off to college and taken separate paths. Life was like that. What was once so close and important eventually became so strange and different.

Like right now.

The priest finished his prayer and gazed at the assembled guests. "I close with Esmeralda's most beloved quote, the one framed above her desk. '*I do not insist,*' answered Don Quixote, '*that this is a full adventure, but it is the beginning of one, for this is the way adventures begin.*'" The priest paused. "And now, I invite each of you to say goodbye."

Jocasta let out a wrenching wail.

Cassiopeia wrapped her arm around her best friend's shoulder and drew her close. As much as Cassiopeia would miss this larger than life amazing woman, her daughter would be bereft in an even deeper way, one Cassiopeia understood all too well. Losing parents was tough. But at least, she thought, Jocasta had not squandered any years with her mother, while Cassiopeia had lost almost a decade with her parents when they experienced their own estrangement. She wondered if Pedro was regretting the years he'd spent halfway across the world, seeing his mother so infrequently. Regrets were both harsh and cruel. Lost moments never to be regained. All of it preyed on the psyche in a way that no amount of justification and rationalization could ever erase.

No way at all.

The coffin began its descent.

Breath caught in her throat.

Esmerelda was gone.

Now resting forever beside her husband, who'd died a long time ago.

The call had come to her chateau in France four days ago. Jocasta barely coherent. Esmerelda had been shot multiple times. She was in surgery, fighting for her life. The doctors tried, but the damage had been too extensive. She died on the operating table, never regaining consciousness. What happened? Who shot her? Why?

After four days, the police still had no answers.

The coffin stopped its descent.

Slowly, in silence, each person approached, bowed their heads, then sprinkled a handful of dirt into the earth. When everyone had finished and moved away, Jocasta and Pedro stood. Together, they began to walk toward the grave. Jocasta stopped and motioned that Cassiopeia should come with them. Pedro nodded his approval, so she came close and took Jocasta's hand. They walked to the grave and tossed their own handful of earth, listening as the soil rained off the coffin's polished surface. In her mind she told Esmerelda she would miss her. But her private goodbye was interrupted by Jocasta, her legs weakening from grief. Cassiopeia reached out and held her friend. Pedro helped too. Jocasta grabbed hold of herself and said she'd be fine. They lingered a few more moments then began the walk to the waiting limousine.

She and Jocasta climbed inside.

"Do you want me to ask Pedro if he needs a ride?" she asked.

Jocasta shook her head. "He got here on his own. He'll find his way."

Apparently their emotional truce had ended with the funeral. She decided not to press the issue. Now was not the time.

The car headed off, back to Esmerelda's house in the hills to greet the mourners.

"So many people came," Jocasta said, as they rode.

"She was loved."

"The service was beautiful."

Cassiopeia nodded. All true. And meaningless.

Jocasta slipped off her sunglasses and turned to Cassiopeia, her eyes red and swollen from crying. "Who would want to shoot my mother?"

The first time Jocasta had broached this subject.

Perhaps now, after the burial, she was ready to face reality.

Cassiopeia had spoken to the police. Esmerelda had been shot at her car, in the parking lot of her law office, around eleven P.M. five nights ago. Robbery was the first thought. But nothing had been taken from her purse, nor the purse itself, which had been an expensive Chanel clutch. The car, a high-end Volvo, had not been taken either, though the key had been right there. With that motive eliminated, the police had turned to Esmerelda's client list, searching for someone that might have a grudge to bear.

"The police have learned nothing so far," she said. "No witnesses. No evidence. Nothing."

"What are you going to do about it?" Jocasta asked. Direct. And to the point. "You have the means, ability, and skills to find out what happened. Do something."

True, she'd been involved in some fairly high-stakes exploits, some of which Jocasta knew about. They'd had conversations on the subject over the past few months. She'd jumped out of airplanes, avoided explosives, been chased in cars, and shot at more times than she could remember. She knew how to handle a gun, deal with pressure, and get herself out of trouble. About the only thing that got to her was high places. Not a full-fledged fear of heights, but about as close as one could get. She also had a friendly relationship with ex-American president Danny Daniels. Not to mention many European law enforcement people.

So her reply was never in doubt.

"I plan to do just that."

Chapter Two

MONDAY

ROBERT TRAVERS APPRECIATED THE SEA, AND THE WATER IN THE CALM Mediterranean seemed to be quite accommodating. Tiny swells. Not much more than a five-knot wind out of the north.

His boat was sleek and stylish. Like a spaceship. With a striking white hull, lots of shiny glass windows, and a helicopter pad toward its bow. A hundred and fifty meters long. One of the largest private yachts in the world. Intentionally, a mid-20th century style dominated, as he loved that time period. Pared-back. Curvaceous. Nostalgic. An array of flowing shapes with none of the wood veneers that were once popular, like glossy teak or shiny mahogany. Everything here was a textural timber. Lots of beech, birch, and pine, which brought an even more contemporary feel.

Painted on its stern was a name. *Sanctuaire.* Sanctuary.

Perfect. As this was his.

During one of their last arguments before the divorce, his second wife accused him of loving the ship more than her. *It's an extension of you,* she'd mused. Actually, she had it backward. He was an extension of the ship. Part of its array of physicality—just like his art collection, guns, antique musical instruments, and rare books. All of the things that made him who he was. Along with about eight hundred million euros in liquid wealth.

He was a man to be feared and respected. Not to be taken lightly.

A person who would never stand for being shamed or dishonored.

Ever.

He savored a last drag of the cigar, then flicked the remnant out over the stern rail into the ship's frothy wake.

His insides churned like the sea.

But at least things were now in motion.

Cassiopeia Vitt owed him a great debt he intended to collect in full, and the first installment, the brutal murder of Esmerelda Fortuna, had been acquired.

He was protective of *his* things. Like his three sons. Ages nine, twelve, and fifteen. They'd come late in life for him and lived with his fourth wife, Celine, in Andorra. They'd been married for sixteen years, a record for him. But the union endured only because Celine asked nothing other than financial support and a token show of civility.

Both of which he gladly provided.

She stayed in Andorra, rarely venturing from the estate. He lived on the ship, sailing on international waters ninety percent of the time. He visited her every few months, no more than a day or so, with no pattern and never long enough for his enemies to know he was there. Once upon a time he'd thought a wife needed to be someone he could show off at Cannes or in Monaco at the Grand Prix. A woman whose looks and glamour signaled he had what it took to attract her.

And he'd had those.

But those marriages never lasted, each one collapsing from the weight of its own pretentiousness. Age finally taught him that he needed a wife who wanted a family and didn't care if it ruined her figure. A solid, practical soul who understood that men like him could never be caged, so why try. Celine had been the perfect choice. She wanted children, not romance. Security, not fidelity. Money, but not for herself, though she lived well, but rather to take care of her sons and the elderly grandparents who'd raised her. She'd grown up on the edge of poverty and never wanted to experience that misery again. So if her husband wanted to spend three quarters of his time on a ship—alone or with *friends*, as she called them—that was a fair exchange. Though overall he had a low opinion of women, he actually admired Celine and sometimes felt a little guilty when he took advantage of her generosity.

Just a little, though.

And the feeling always passed.

Though he was nearing eighty, he looked and acted like a man twenty years younger. He was beefy, but with toned muscle not fat, thanks to daily workouts. He had a full head of wavy silver hair and curious dark, almost black, eyes. A thick gold chain stayed around his neck and a diamond Franck Muller watch wrapped his left wrist, one of many from his extensive collection. His pressed white slacks, white shirt, and blue deck shoes matched the yacht's color scheme, which he liked to wear while on board.

He turned from the stern rail and gazed across the deck at the woman lounging on one of the recliners.

Francesca was twenty-six and regularly walked the runways for Dolce & Gabbana, Gucci, and Chanel. She was a natural blonde, with not a blemish on her rail-thin body. Quiet and reserved in public, in bed she enjoyed playing dangerous games.

Which he liked.

"Are you coming with me?" he asked her, walking over. "The plane is waiting at the Nice airport to take me to Geneva. My meeting will take only a few hours."

Going ashore came with risks. At least three governments were actively investigating him on charges that ranged from bribery, to corruption, to extortion. No formal charges had been issued, and none of it would ever stick. But he detested the constant aggravation along with paying lawyers to make it all go away. So he tried to limit his visits ashore to only countries that were friendly and amiable.

Like France, Italy, and Switzerland.

"I don't think so," she said. "I have a busy week coming up. I think I'll stay here and enjoy the sun."

She wore practically nothing, the micro bikini living up to its name.

"And maybe plan a surprise for you after dinner, when you return." She tossed him a quick smile. "Would you like that?"

"I would not." He bent down and untied the yellow bows on her bikini top. "I'd actually adore it." He freed the offending garment from her pale skin and dropped it to the deck.

She seemed to like his advances.

He massaged her small, firm breasts.

She arched her back, inviting more. She had a penchant for the kind of rough play that so few women, to his experience, really enjoyed.

"Take off my bottom," she told him.

He untied the little bows at either hip. When he reached for her, she shook her head and sat up in the recliner, a leg extended out on either side.

"Not yet," she said. "On your knees, and ask for what you want."

He allowed the delicious thrill of a beautiful woman ordering him around to sweep through him. Plenty of women pretended to like the game to get what he had to offer outside of the bedroom. But only a few played it right. True, Francesca enjoyed his gifts, but she did not need them. She made a seven-figure income on her own. Money was not one of her wants.

Instead, she just loved to play.

She particularly liked making him do her bidding.

And he liked doing it.

He stepped from the shower, satisfied with the sex that had ended a few minutes ago. Francesca had offered to join him under the hot water, but he'd had enough of her for one day. No sense allowing her to think he craved it. Because he didn't. Take it or leave it. Either worked for him. Thankfully he was in a position to take what he wanted, when he wanted.

He walked into his stateroom and dressed. Beige slacks, Gucci loafers, a white button-down shirt, and a pale green vicuña sweater that he knotted around his neck. He owned a few suits but couldn't remember the last time he'd worn one. He detested neckties. He liked going casual, especially if everyone else was in business attire. It singled him out. Made him different. But mostly he just liked doing what he wanted. Money and influence offered him that luxury, with few questions asked.

And he particularly hated questions.

Francesca wasn't on deck when he departed. He left word with the majordomo that he'd be back by seven P.M. and climbed down into the sleek Mercedes-Benz AMG cigarette racing craft that he used as a ship-to-shore ferry. No need for the helicopter today, which rested safely in its bay toward the ship's bow. Besides—

Who didn't like being hauled around in a two-million-dollar boat.

Three hours later he walked into his Swiss banker's office. He'd always admired the elegant simplicity and monochromatic décor. Minimalism at its most ostentatiousness. Its tall plate-glass windows opened to a spectacular view of Lake Geneva.

Paul Bixel rose to greet him. An academic-looking man with thinning brown hair, hooded eyes, and when he offered it, a narrow, almost crooked smile. Any sense of humor, if it existed, had remained hidden for all the time Travers had known him. He read the concerned expression without Bixel having to say a word. Whatever residual exhilaration he'd felt from the morning's encounter with Francesca had evaporated on the short hop west from Venice.

This place was always about bad news.

He sat down across from his old friend.

He knew the purpose of the meeting. He was being sued by an array of former clients, many of them the kind of people who could not be bullied nor ignored. Important people who possessed power and influence similar to his. So he was trying to settle the disputes out of court to everyone's satisfaction. The issues presented by each case were ultra-sensitive and could not be discussed on open ship-to-shore communication lines. These had to be addressed face to face, behind closed doors. This was the tenth in a series of meetings that had occurred over the last few months.

"Do you have the final figures on what this is going to cost me?" he asked Bixel.

No preamble, no niceties. He was not the kind of man inclined to waste time on formalities or small talk.

"You're not going to like it."

"Of course I'm not going to like it. But is there a choice?"

He knew Bixel came from wealth. His grandfather had started the bank, one of hundreds of private financial institutions scattered across Switzerland, which offered a variety of services to discerning clients willing to pay the astronomical fees. Bixel had been involved with the Repository from the start, a private safe deposit vault for the über-wealthy that Travers had created within the principality of Andorra. It had sheltered precious metals, art, jewelry, stockpiles of cash, gold, silver, and platinum. Overtaxing governments, worry about world stock markets, concerns about the threat of a global recession and climate change had, over the last decade, made safe havens like the Repository more necessary than ever. His had been quite popular. Every subterranean vault had been leased out on a long-term basis. It had been a state-of-the-art facility hidden beneath La Vasari Biblioteca, a 19th-century edifice nestled deep in an Andorran forest. A hugely successful venture, making him millions of legal euros annually.

Until a few months ago.

When it all came crashing down.

Law enforcement appeared. Searches made. Property confiscated. Governments intervened. Then the taxing authorities arrived. The lawsuits came last, about fifty so far, and he'd been forced to pay off each plaintiff, settling their claims, obtaining ironclad nondisclosure agreements.

But a few holdouts remained.

Which Bixel and the lawyers had been trying to resolve.

"It's going to take nearly a hundred million euros to shut the rest up," Bixel said. "I know this is more than we estimated, but people are taking advantage of the situation. They know you can't engage in a prolonged legal fight. You can't even appear in court. So we have little leverage. As of yesterday, we've finished negotiating all but nine of the lawsuits. We're confident we can get those to come around."

He really could not blame any of the plaintiffs. Their secrecy and confidentiality had been grievously exposed. Many of them were facing legal action, both civilly and criminally, from governments around the world. Mainly over taxes that were never paid on hidden assets. One of the plaintiffs had already been indicted for fraud in England and was facing jail. He'd considered using violence to end the problem but rejected the idea since there would surely be retaliation. No sense risking that when money could solve things.

The whole idea of the Repository had been for it to remain secret. But one person had destroyed all that.

Cassiopeia Vitt.

She'd brought it all down in order to find some paintings that her father had left her in his will.

"Pay them off and get it done," he said.

"I can do that. But what are you going to do?"

This man knew him well. Maybe too well. But the more time he spent in the world of the establishment, the more he felt disconnected from it. He hated the manners and customs. The rules and regulations. The rights and wrongs. For him, only power mattered.

"It's not what am I going to do. It's what I *am* doing. I assure you, Paul, the person who created all this turmoil will rue the day she ever crossed me."

Chapter Three

WEDNESDAY

CASSIOPEIA WAS BACK HOME IN FRANCE, AT GIVORS.

She'd spent Monday with Jocasta, then left yesterday afternoon. Her old friend had assured her she was going to be okay. Once home, she'd made herself a simple dinner of vegetable soup, with a chunk of a baguette and a glass of wine, retiring to her bed and watching an old 1950's movie to try and take her mind off the last seventy-two hours. *Sabrina*, with Audrey Hepburn and Humphrey Bogart, was her go-to escape whenever she was depressed. She and her mother used to watch it together at least once a year, enamored with the style, the glamour, Hepburn's gamine charm and Bogart's gruff descent into romance. Old movies were one of their shared mother-daughter delights, and last night, missing Esmerelda, she'd found herself missing her mother too. The two women had been best of friends.

Now they both were gone.

After the movie ended she'd tried, but failed, to fall asleep. She kept thinking about Jocasta's unwillingness to deal with her brother. He'd tried repeatedly to approach her, but Jocasta had snubbed every effort. Not having any siblings, she'd encouraged Jocasta to mend the rift. They were the only family they each had left. But she'd refused. Whatever happened between them had been bad.

Really bad.

She'd finally drifted off into a nightmare-filled sleep and woke up later than usual, still tired. She thought about taking a long run, except it was Wednesday, which meant she had her weekly meeting with Viktor Olsen starting in an hour.

She could never have undertaken such a gargantuan construction project without him. Givors was an ancient French town that evolved into an important medieval enclave. Its teardrop-shaped center was still entered through two 14th century gates, designed far more for decoration than defense. Two unremarkable churches lined the main square, along with houses of wood and stone, the majority now filled with cafés and shops. Most of its inhabitants lived then, and now, in the forests beyond. Her chateau was one of many constructed long ago, maintained through a succession of dedicated owners, she being the latest. Her reconstruction project was aimed at reviving one of the region's oldest castles. The masoned tower near the parking lot that greeted visitors said it all.

WELCOME TO THE PAST. HERE AT GIVORS, A SITE ONCE OCCUPIED BY LOUIS IX, A CASTLE IS BEING CONSTRUCTED USING MATERIALS AND TECHNIQUES ONLY AVAILABLE TO 13TH CENTURY CRAFTSMEN. A MASONED TOWER WAS THE VERY SYMBOL OF A LORD'S POWER. THE CASTLE AT GIVORS WAS DESIGNED AS A MILITARY FORTRESS WITH THICK WALLS AND CORNER TOWERS. THE SURROUNDING ENVIRONS PROVIDED AN ABUNDANCE OF WATER, STONE, EARTH, SAND, AND WOOD, WHICH WERE ALL NEEDED FOR ITS CONSTRUCTION. QUARRIERS, STONE HEWERS, MASONS, CARPENTERS, BLACKSMITHS, AND POTTERS ARE NOW LABORING, LIVING AND DRESSING EXACTLY AS THEY WOULD HAVE EIGHT CENTURIES AGO. THE PROJECT IS PRIVATELY FUNDED AND THE CURRENT ESTIMATE IS 20 YEARS WILL BE NEEDED TO COMPLETE THE CASTLE. ENJOY YOUR TIME IN THE 13TH CENTURY.

She employed one hundred and twenty men and women who worked at the site year round. The costs were enormous. Luckily her parents left her both a fortune and the ownership of one of Europe's largest conglomerates, *Terra*, which dealt in coal, minerals, precious metals, and rare gems. It supplied everything from high-end electronics to parts for planes and missiles. Demand never seemed to cease. Over the past decade, the people who ran the corporation had doubled its net worth. She was a billionaire several times over, proud that she was putting some of that capital to good historical use.

She and Viktor had attended university together, both working on architectural degrees, hers with a specialty in medieval history. During their second year she'd shared her dream of rebuilding a medieval castle and that she had the means to make it happen. Five years after they'd graduated, she'd invited him to come on board and he'd agreed. They made a good team. She produced the initial designs—

And Viktor changed them.

Usually for the better.

She waited in her office at 8:15 with a pot of strong coffee, some fresh croissants, and raspberry jam made on site. She was pouring her second cup when Viktor arrived. She offered him some, but he said he'd had too much already this morning.

"We had some trouble Monday," he said.

She never liked the sound of that. "Why didn't you contact me?"

"It was late in the day when you returned yesterday, and you need to see this in person. Let's take a walk and I'll explain."

They left the study and strolled across the chateau grounds toward the construction site and a small admin center that helped educate visitors about what life had been like in Gaul over seven hundred years ago. Some lauded her building efforts as an important contribution to the study of civilization. Others labeled it a folly. A waste of resources. But she'd made it her life's work and was proud of it.

"We had a summer school visit Monday," Viktor said. "A small group of seventh graders broke away from their class and took off on their own. Their teacher was frantic. They were missing for over four hours."

She was shocked.

Viktor nodded. "I know. It was serious and frightening. We shut the admin center down, and I enlisted every employee to help in the search."

They'd reached the castle and entered, walking through the grand hall, its roofless four stone walls towering over ten meters. He led her down one corridor, then another, and out a rear exit, heading for an area that was usually closed to the public.

And for good reason.

She'd built the castle on land that had not only once housed another castle but also a series of *erdstalls*. Tunnels of unknown origin that most believed dated to the Dark Ages. Usually low and narrow, winding through the ground like a maze. Why did they exist? Nobody really knew for sure. The most prominent theory was they provided some sort of religious purpose. They were particularly common in Bavaria and Austria, but had been found all over Europe, including France. Her team had managed to make some cursory explorations and learned that one tributary led to the basement of the original castle. A few of the other routes led in and out from the castle walls. A majority of the tunnels remained a mystery as they had not, as yet, been thoroughly mapped. Exploring the *erdstalls* was dangerous for a variety of reasons. They could collapse. There could be blockages. Flooding. So they'd sealed them off with warning signs.

"Did they go into the tunnels?" she asked.

He nodded. "They ignored the barriers. Or rather I should say they went around a barrier."

Ahead she saw that one of the four boulders lying in front of the entrance to an *erdstall* had been slid aside from its neighbor just enough to allow someone to slip past. The stones were massive. They'd used a pulley system to roll them into place, which had taken several men. The barrier was critical to ensuring people would not venture inside.

"How could they have moved this rock?" she asked.

"They didn't."

She was confused.

"Follow me."

She skirted around and into the tunnel. A waft of wet sandstone and damp earth filled her nostrils. The smell of age and mystery, she liked to say. She followed Viktor for about thirty meters. The ceiling was low enough that she had to squat. Viktor, even more so.

"Did anyone talk to the children?" she asked.

"Security spent a long time with them."

"And did they get an explanation?"

She kept following him deeper into the earth. Good thing Cotton wasn't here. He hated confined spaces. Even she was feeling a little uneasy.

"It's not the kids," he said. "It's what they found that's the problem."

He turned down one of the tributaries. The tunnel began to narrow even further, but they kept going. Finally, Viktor stopped and focused the flashlight beam on the rock wall, where she saw fresh excavations. Cavities chopped into the tunnel wall. Eight. No. Ten. The mandate at Givors was to avoid modern tools and technology while constructing the castle. In the decade since she'd started they'd managed to stay true to those goals. These niches had come from modern steel picks and shovels.

"What are they?" she asked.

"I don't know. I only know they're fresh."

She stared at the violations.

"When we found the kids, we found these too," he said. "They didn't do this. So we staked out the tunnels for the past two nights to see if anyone returned. No one did."

"Are you going to watch again tonight?"

He nodded. "Something's going on."

And she agreed.

Cassiopeia exited the tunnels and headed back across the grounds to her office.

Her cell phone rang.

A quick glance at the screen and she saw it was Cotton. She retreated to the shade of a willow tree and leaned against the thick trunk.

"Do you have a few minutes to talk?" he asked her when she answered.

His voice, with that slight drawl, made her feel instantly warm, like always.

"Absolutely," she said.

They talked every day, and she'd already worked through the funeral and its aftermath with him. He too was ready to join in any investigation of Esmerelda's murder. But they'd both agreed to give the police a little time to make some progress before interfering. She'd established a solid contact with the *Guardia Civil* who were handling the case and planned to head back to Spain early next week.

"There's been a change of plans about me coming to Givors," he said.

She didn't like to hear that. He was supposed to come tomorrow and spend a week. They alternated back and forth between France and Denmark with their regular visits.

"Stephanie asked me to fill in for her at a ceremony in San Marino."

He'd once worked for Stephanie Nelle as one of her agents at the Magellan Billet, an investigative arm of the United States Justice Department that Stephanie both created and headed. She'd chosen him as one of her first recruits and, when he retired out early, she'd continued to call on him for special assignments. At the moment Stephanie was in hot water with the current American president, suspended from her job, pending a hearing on her termination. So Cassiopeia understood. No way Stephanie could attend anything official.

"I'm not canceling without a plan," he said to her.

That was good to hear.

"I'll go to San Marino on Saturday and do my duty. You fly over too. There's a really lovely stretch of Italian beach not far from there with a marvelous hotel. Do you know the area?"

She did, having visited the microstate of San Marino before. One of the world's smallest countries and, as it proudly proclaimed, the oldest surviving sovereign state. Just sixty-one square kilometers, home to 34,000 people. It sat in the Apennine mountain range, along the slope of Monte Titano. An enclave of hilly topography totally surrounded by the Italian territories of Emilia-Romagna and Marche. A place rich with history and heritage. As a child, she and her parents had hiked all over it and visited each of the three castle-like citadels. Lots of fond memories had come from that place.

She also knew about Cotton's connection.

A few months back the Germanisches Nationalmuseum, in Nuremberg, had decided to repatriate a hundred and five works of art to their rightful homes. Included were several gold pieces from the famed Domagnano Treasure that the museum was returning to San Marino. The Ostrogothic hoard of gold objects had been found in the late 19th century in San Marino. Two dozen pieces of jewelry from the 5th and 6th centuries that may have belonged to a noble lady of high rank. Earrings, pendants, necklaces, rings, even a gold hairpin. Eventually, the bulk of the treasure wound up in Germany, with other pieces scattered between New York's Metropolitan Museum of Art, the British Museum, and the Louvre Abu Dhabi. En route back to San Marino, the twenty-four gold objects were stolen. As a favor to a friend who was high up in the German office of Culture, Stephanie Nelle had agreed to investigate the robbery, and Cotton had found the stolen merchandise.

"The government of San Marino has an annual summer festival that falls this weekend, and they asked Stephanie to be part of the festivities. She obviously can't, and I couldn't tell her no. So I'm going to fill in on Saturday. The ceremony starts at noon, and I'm told it will be over by one. So I can meet you after that at the Rimini Riviera for some swimming, eating, and other things. You've had a rough week, and I'm guessing you could use a few days of peace."

He was right.

"That sounds perfect," she said. "I'll see you there."

Chapter Four

TRAVERS HAD AWOKEN IN A FOUL MOOD.

He was an extremely wealthy man. More than enough money for several lifetimes. And he'd been known to waste some of that fortune on frivolity. But he could afford to. What he hated, though, was failing. Even worse—someone else had actually caused the failure and just walked away.

That was intolerable.

The morning loomed the color of lead. Storm clouds hung over *Sanctuaire* and only served to exacerbate his anger. Yesterday, he'd received more bad news. Another of the Repository's clients had refused to settle, claiming that the breach in security had placed his entire business reputation in jeopardy. Andorra was a notorious tax haven. The scandal had cast negative aspersions on him, so he was suing Travers for a loss of income. The worst part was the idiot was going public in the media with his accusations, claiming the only way to prove he was not hiding assets was to not hide anything at all.

Like that was going to work.

Good old Irish rage seethed through him.

He'd been born near Cork on the southwest coast and made a fortune shipping durable goods to Africa and the Middle East. Eventually, he metamorphized those trade routes into arms dealing, beginning in the 1970s, brokering deals between American manufacturers and the Saudi Arabian government. Lockheed Martin had paid him over a hundred million dollars in commissions for those sales. He later worked with other American, French, and Israeli corporations to broker more lucrative deals. He'd even acquired a nickname. The Leprechaun. The guy with the pot of gold. His company, Viking Traders, a Luxembourg entity, now dealt exclusively in global weaponry, including small arms, tanks, fighter planes, even ballistic missiles.

All of it legal.

But all that depended on discretion.

He was the quintessential middleman, negotiating deals that allowed buyers and sellers a high degree of anonymity, and he provided that insulation.

It was the side ventures that had kept him in trouble with countries around the world. Corruption. Bribery. Extortion. Even some human trafficking, which he'd found most profitable. All necessary evils in the world in which he lived, where excess was king and nothing was off limits.

He'd always been something of a playboy. A Wikipedia page, not all that authoritative as far as he was concerned, indicated four marriages and some questionable relationships with young women. Two of those relationships had resulted in legal problems, but nothing was noted as to their outcome. Certainly a man with his reputation attracted trouble. And nobody bought a ship the size of a destroyer, and avoided every country's territorial waters, for no reason.

But the Repository?

That had opened him up to unparalleled public scrutiny and liability.

More than he ever imagined.

His instinct was to find Francesca and blow off some steam in bed. But she'd left early to go ashore and was not due back for a few hours. Maybe he should go ashore too. Women were easy to find, and a little variety might be a nice change of pace. So he picked up the ship's phone and informed the captain to arrange for the boat to take him into town.

He grabbed a shower and shaved.

Routine always brought comfort. The way he lathered his face, the razor scrapping a long path through the thick cream, the image of himself that appeared on the mirror, steamed by the hot water. He liked what he saw, as would the woman he'd soon find. His spirits rose with the anticipation, the entire experience of getting ready settling his nerves. He dressed, but as he walked out on deck to leave, the sky opened up and rain poured down.

Damn. He hated storms.

Especially ones with thunder.

Where others found it soothing or comforting, he just felt anxious. Sometimes even trembling, sweating, or panicking unnecessarily. A few times he even cried, though no one had ever seen that happen. All ironic for someone who loved the sea and had spent most of his adult life living on a ship.

His affliction even had a fancy name.

Astraphobia.

He'd spent hundreds of thousands of dollars with therapists to learn that label and find some relief. They'd all told him that reassurance from other people was good, being alone bad. But there was no way anyone was going to see him when the effects took hold. One even suggested that he hide underneath a bed, or under the covers, in a closet, or some other confined space where he might feel safer. Something about the claustrophobia might help.

But that wasn't going to happen either.

He was obsessed with weather forecasts, always on the alert for incoming storms. Today's forecast had come with only a thirty percent chance of rain. And while the specialists had been able to confirm his diagnosis, they'd not been able to offer any definitive help with the panic attacks. Most just told him that the more he experienced storms the more immunity he'd build. One moron even suggested he stand in the rain and repeat phrases to himself in order to be calm, maybe add some breathing exercises to reinforce things.

Really? Like that was going to happen.

He watched the rain from the aft deck and fought the memories that lived coiled in the dark recesses of his mind. No matter how hard he tried to forget, there would always be a child inside him who'd watched his drunken father throw his mother through a window. Which had allowed the rain inside, soaking him from the storm that had raged that day. He'd stared as the water diluted the blood to the faintest of pink, huddled under that broken window watching his mother bleed to death. Quite a sight for a six-year-old. Wet and shivering. He waited there beside her until the police arrived the next morning, after finding his father drowned in a nearby lake.

He didn't speak a word for nearly six months.

His grandparents tried to raise him, but they could not exorcise the demons that had rooted themselves deep inside him. Demons that were still there, despite being nearly eighty years old.

He sucked in several deep breaths, turned his back on the rain, and descended into the bowels of the ship to the one place he retreated to when upset. The one place that did offer comfort.

The music room.

Many spaces on board cast musical themes. Lautrec posters of dance halls in the study. Degas paintings of ballet dancers for the dining room. A collection of ancient flutes displayed in the main salon. The music room covered the full spectrum, dedicated to it all.

His mother had been a talented violinist. Not orchestra quality or anything like that. Just good. Music truly soothed her sad soul.

His too.

He liked the music room for not only how it reminded him of her, but it was one of the few spaces without portholes, hermetically sealed and temperature controlled because it housed his world-class collection of violins and guitars. Rooms cut off from storms definitely helped with the anxiety brought on by astraphobia. He knew exactly why he had the affliction, just not how to get rid of it. But did he really want to? It seemed the last tenuous connection to a woman long dead.

He unlocked the door and entered the music room.

On occasion he'd been known to show off his collection. What was the point of owning such magnificent musical instruments if others could not appreciate them? But he was careful, as the provenance of many of the pieces was questionable.

He switched on the lights and admired the plexiglass-fronted cases. His nerves were calming down now that he was away from the rain. He was both a collector and an amateur luthier. He owned all of the requite tools and materials necessary to repair and restore guitars and violins. A sense of peace came when he worked with wood, sandpaper, and shellacs. Perhaps if life had been different, if his mother had not been murdered, if she'd not been drawn to an asshole of a man, he might have become a professional luthier.

Not wealthy, but satisfied.

Not powerful, but calm.

Lying on the workbench was a 1959 Martin guitar he'd been working on for several weeks. He switched on the room's stereo system, which blared out Beethoven's Fifth symphony. Now he could no longer hear nor feel the storm.

The ship road steady in the churning water.

He wasn't going ashore today, so he settled down to work.

Restringing was the last step in any restoration. It could be aggravating, but he liked the distraction. He'd just begun to secure the second of six strings when his phone rang. He checked, then tapped the screen and answered the call on speaker.

"We have a new development," Paul Bixel said.

"I'm listening."

He tightened the string.

"Three more lawsuits have come in."

"You said everything had been filed that was going to be filed."

"I thought it was, but the press attention has given—"

"Find someone to handle the media," he yelled. "Get it done. Hire the best PR firm in the world for damage control. Do it."

He kept tightening the string, but his rising anger caused him to overtighten, and it popped with a loud ping.

Dammit.

"I'll not be embarrassed and humiliated like this anymore," he said to the phone. "Having to pay off clients quietly is one thing, but to have stories circulating in the world media about me being sued. That's intolerable. The people I deal with, Paul, will not want to deal with me anymore. They function in a world of discretion and secrecy." His voice kept rising. "Not media and the internet. I can't allow this to continue. It has to end." He stopped working on the strings and stared at the phone. "I will not have everything I've ever done rendered useless because of one damn woman. Do. You. Understand?"

"I do."

"Then get to work," he said. "Do your job, and I'll do mine."

He ended the call and found a chamois to wipe away the fingerprints he'd left on the guitar's glassy surface.

A few strokes and they disappeared.

Not a trace remained.

Just like Cassiopeia Vitt.

In just a short while.

Chapter Five

THURSDAY

CASSIOPEIA SAT AT HER DESK AND THUMBED THROUGH APPLICATIONS from around the world. Typically, each year, she hosted a half-dozen graduate archaeology candidates to live and work at the construction site. They helped excavate and catalog the remnants of the former castle and received academic credit at their respective universities. Choosing among the candidates was one of her favorite exercises, and this latest group of applicants seemed particularly well qualified.

A distant explosion rocked the morning.

She looked up from the paper in her hand. Blasting was not part of the repertoire used at the construction site, as that technique had not been available in the 13th century. It was sometimes utilized at the quarry, though, but that was a few kilometers away and certainly not ever used at 7:30 in the morning.

She sprang from her desk and opened the French doors, stepping out onto the terrace. Panic set in when she saw a dust cloud rising from the construction site. She ran toward it, down the service road, about a hundred meters. Ahead, people were fleeing the partially completed castle.

"What happened?" she asked them, approaching.

"An explosion and a wall collapsed," one of those leaving told her.

The castle walls were all designed to be tall and several meters thick. But in their infancy they were quite fragile and could fall. That was why timber supports were used to hold them upright for a time.

She headed onto the site.

It seemed that everything had occurred in an area off the grand hall which had walls but no ceiling. The air was thick with dust, and she had trouble breathing and seeing. Debris was everywhere. A dozen or so workers and students lay on the ground. Viktor was squatting, talking to one of them. She made her way over and stopped to check on the first person she reached, one of the archeologists, who was bleeding from a gash to his forehead. She ripped off her scarf and applied it to the wound, telling him to hold it tight. Beside him, one of the artists was holding an arm to her side.

"I was thrown back and landed on it," she said.

"Can you move it?"

"Barely."

She hustled off toward Viktor, checking on more of the wounded. It seemed like a lot of injury, but nothing overly serious or life threatening.

Which was good.

"Were ambulances called?" she asked Viktor.

He nodded. "Along with police and fire department."

A phone rang.

Viktor's.

He checked the screen and mouthed that he needed to take it. She nodded and headed to the blast site where some of her team members stood staring at the gaping hole in the ground and the collapsed wall. Chunks of stone, which had taken months to quarry and hewn, lay in piles.

"We need water, first aid kits, and blankets," she told them.

But no one moved.

"Adam, Peter, go get water," she yelled. "Emily, the first aid kits."

They seemed to grab hold of themselves and scattered.

She made her way back to Viktor, who was still on his phone. He was telling the security people to clear the grounds of all visitors and direct traffic away from the main gate so the emergency crews would not be stalled.

He ended the call.

"What happened?" she asked.

"It was an explosion. Out of nowhere, from underground. Right below one of the walls, which instantly collapsed. No warning, no time to do anything. Thankfully, no one was actually standing near the wall or over that crater."

Thank goodness.

"Cassiopeia," he said. "I stationed Jean Claude at the tunnel entrance last night to keep guard. Like we discussed. We can't find him. I've sent security to search."

She heard the concern in his voice.

They prided themselves on running a safe construction site, with strict rules and regulations that went above and beyond required safety measures. And though they used olden techniques, that did not mean safety took a back seat. They'd had their share of injuries, but none had been due to wantonness or gross negligence.

And they'd never had a fatality.

"What's happening here?" she asked.

The idea of sabotage seemed frightening. Who? Why? This was an archeological site. Nothing more.

Within fifteen minutes police, paramedics, and the fire department arrived. The medics examined those who'd been injured, while the police inspected the crater. Her own people reported on the physical damage done to the castle. Three walls had fallen, which would require new stones from the quarry and a total rebuild.

"If you ask me," Viktor said. "Somebody intentionally set a bomb."

She was rapidly coming to the same conclusion, particularly after learning about the trespass into the tunnels beneath the site.

Something was definitely happening here.

Somebody would only purposefully destroy an historical site for one reason. Revenge. A disgruntled employee? Maybe. But their turnover rate was negligible, and everyone who'd left had done so on good terms. Not a single name came to mind.

But something else did.

Esmerelda and Givors.

Two things near and dear to her.

Both attacked. Coincidence? No way.

One of the masons came running to where she and Viktor were standing.

"We think we know where Jean Claude is," the man said, though out of breath. "He's trapped in the tunnels."

Chapter Six

Travers sat up in bed.

The room was pitch dark thanks to the blackout curtains. Every stateroom on the ship had them. He glanced at the bedside table and the digital clock. 8:04 A.M. He'd slept in short bursts amongst an array of dreaming. Loud. In color. With movement. He wondered how the human brain managed such a feat. Movies in the mind. His own brain seemed to have no problem producing them. Never had he had any issues with sleeping—until the past few months.

He swung around and sat on the edge of the bed, inserting his feet into slippers. Beside him, Francesca stirred and opened her eyes.

"Are you coming back?" she asked.

"I don't think so. I have work to do."

She reached over and touched him. "What's wrong? You haven't been yourself for days."

He stood and shrugged on his bathrobe. "Go back to sleep. I'm going to be working all day. If you want to take the boat to shore, you might enjoy yourself more than being here."

"Should I be worried?"

He did not turn back and face her. "I don't want anyone ever to be worried for me. I'm fully in control, Francesca. As always."

But he didn't feel in control.

And that was the problem.

Rage was driving him.

Which wasn't a bad thing.

He'd taken down enemies on more than one occasion, through legal and illegal means. Some in anger, most in a dead calm. He'd never tolerated even the tiniest of slights. His reputation was one of a man not to cross.

Yet he had been crossed.

By a rich Spanish woman named Cassiopeia Vitt.

He walked to his study and switched on the Keurig. He dropped a pod into the slot and listened as the machine kicked into action. He wasn't supposed to drink more than three cups of coffee a day. Screw the doctors. He'd gotten this far ignoring them, so he wasn't about to start listening to them now.

He retrieved the steaming mug and sat at his desk. A quick check of the e-mails which had come in since last evening revealed the one he'd been waiting for.

Finally.

He sipped the burning, bitter brew, which energized him.

His phone vibrated. He checked the screen and saw a text, which he tapped open.

A sunny day today.

He smiled. Code for "Cassiopeia Vitt's castle reconstruction project had just suffered a major setback."

He smiled, feeling better already.

Part two. Done.

He opened the e-mail and saw there were four attachments. All maps. Of San Marino and its environs. They'd come in through a secured server, obtained by a hired operative on the ground in Italy. He opened the files and studied the geography, his mind churning. He imagined himself on Saturday traversing the ramparts and finding the right parapet.

Esmerelda Fortuna? Dead.

A castle project in France? Destroyed.

Harold Earl "Cotton" Malone, retired agent from the United States Justice Department?

Soon to be dead.

But there was another task to accomplish beforehand.

He grabbed the ship's phone and dialed the extension. His assistant answered after one ring.

"Come to my office. Now," he said.

The hasty summons rang of arrogance and self-satisfaction.

Nothing new for him.

Lucian arrived within two minutes, wearing his usual uniform of chinos and a navy polo shirt. The younger man had the build of an athlete, with sharp, clean features, a cleft chin, icy blue eyes, and a streak of white down one side of his pale brown hair. Lucian had worked for him a long time, their lack of morals and values identical. If he trusted anyone on the planet it was Lucian. Of course, he paid him extremely well and allowed him the run of the ship. Lucian opened his laptop and sat opposite Travers' desk.

"Now that we know the when and where, we have to figure out the particulars on how," he said. "The maps have arrived."

They'd discussed all this before, weighing the various options.

"Have you decided," Lucian asked, "if you want to take care of it before, during, or after?"

He thought, then smiled. "During seems best."

"At what point?"

"Toward the middle. Long enough for everyone to become relaxed." He paused. "That will give us plenty of time to make our retreat." He paused. "Are you ready?"

Lucian nodded. "I've practiced quite a bit. I'm ready."

"You handled Esmerelda Fontana expertly. I have every confidence you'll do the same here."

He sipped more of the coffee, which had not cooled.

The doorknob rattled.

His gaze shot across the room just as Francesca entered. Lucian had obviously not locked it.

"I thought you were staying in bed," he said to her.

"After you left, I couldn't sleep. Would you like some breakfast?"

Careful, he told himself. Stay calm. Reveal nothing. "That would be wonderful. Could you have it prepared and ready on the aft deck? I'll be there shortly."

She smiled then left, closing the door behind her.

He saw the concern on Lucian's face.

His assistant was surely thinking the same thing he was.

Had she heard anything?

Chapter Seven

CASSIOPEIA AIMED THE FLASHLIGHT AND STARED AHEAD INTO THE darkness of the tunnel, the same spot where she and Viktor had been yesterday, where the bolder had been moved, opening a way inside.

"Jean Claude was here, on guard last night," Viktor said. "But no one has seen him this morning. Security found nothing."

"You think somebody came back and planted those explosives?" she asked.

"I do."

So did she. "He could be inside there."

The walls and ceiling looked okay. The damage had all occurred further into the *erdstall*. The authorities were waiting for a special team, trained in subterranean work, to arrive from Toulouse. Best guess estimated their arrival at another hour. She held a copy of a 15th century map that she'd acquired a few years ago which detailed the tunnels.

"I'm not waiting," she said.

"I didn't think you would."

He knew her well.

"The whole tunnel system could collapse," Viktor said. "That explosion did some real damage."

"Your warning is noted."

"And he might not even be in there."

Something told her that he was. And in trouble.

Jean Claude had worked at the site for several years. He was a trusted member of the Givors family. She knew his wife and child, who lived nearby.

"He works for me, and I owe him and his family," she said. "Stay here and keep watch. I'm going in."

She'd secured some clean rags which she now wrapped around her mouth and nose for protection. Lots of bad things could be in the air the deeper she went. She aimed the flashlight ahead and plunged into the narrow tunnel. Most experts believed the *erdstalls* had first been dug sometime in the 10th or 11th centuries. But others placed their origins much older. They were all low and narrow, this one about a meter and a half high. They usually connected to a *schlupf,* a lower tunnel, which was even more impassable. Why they had been dug also remained a mystery. If Jean Claude was trapped that deep, getting to him could prove impossible. Even worse, the *erdstalls* usually had only one entry point, with no second exit.

Not much room for error here.

She turned right and headed for the four-way intersection that she knew lay ahead. She came to the junction and studied the map in the flashlight's halogen beam. It had been prepared by a German long ago, so everything was noted in his native language.

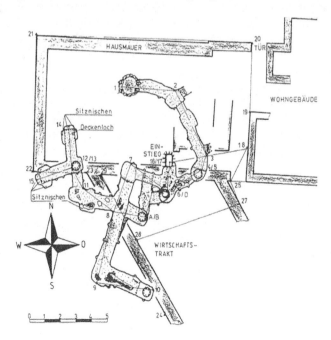

She could go left, right, or straight ahead. Left led to a dead end that barely jutted beneath the old castle walls. Right made its way past the old walls above, deeper into the castle site, toward the grand hall, where the explosion occurred. She gambled that Jean Claude was in that direction. The air was already stale and bitter which raised concerns for toxic mold. In the past, when they'd explored the tunnels, fans had been set up at the entrance to force fresh air through.

Get going, she told herself.

She turned right, then an almost immediate left, stepping ahead with caution, the tunnel here in fairly good shape. A Y-shaped intersection came into view and, from the map, she knew that the offshoot to the right led toward the blast site. Again, amazingly, the *erdstall* had held up to the punishment, though there was more debris here than behind her.

"Jean Claude," she called out.

No reply.

She tried again. Still, only silence.

Little to no archaeological material had ever been found in the tunnels, which had made dating them that much more difficult. Coal from a fire pit found in another of the nearby tunnels had been dated to between 1030 and 1210 A.D. A few ceramic shards pointed to a 12th century origin. All that meant everything around her was uncomfortably old.

It's going to take some time. There's a lot of rubble we'll need to move.

That's what the firemen had told her.

Unfortunately, time was not on Jean Claude's side. Even if he was inside and survived the blast, the air quality was surely compromised with pathogens and carbon dioxide. Hence, why she'd improvised with a mask.

A blockade appeared ahead.

Not bad, but enough that she had to fold the map and put it away, lay the flashlight down, and shift some of the rock and earth behind her, thinning it out down the tunnel's length. No way to just move it aside as the passage was barely a meter wide.

She was beginning to think this was foolish.

But she had to try.

Not her nature to just sit around and wait for others to do

something.

Right? Wrong? It doesn't matter. Just do something. That's what Cotton liked to say, and she agreed. He also had another insult she'd heard him use more than once on himself. *There are two fools in this neighborhood, and I'm both of them.*

Yep.

That was her at the moment.

Another blockage appeared a few meters ahead. She estimated that she was now past the castle's outer wall, somewhere beneath the inner courtyard, headed toward the array of buildings being erected along the north wall, one of which was the grand hall which had been leveled.

She started to work on the next pile. Her nerves were taut, alert, ready for anything. If Jean Claude had descended to the lower tunnels through one of the holes in the earthen floor, he might have had a chance. But the air quality in those was next to nothing. One encouraging fact was that the explosion had exposed the tunnel, and she could see a few shafts of light further down, seeping in.

Where was Jean Claude?

If he'd come this way, where would he be now? She found the map and unfolded it, studying the possibilities with the flashlight. One characteristic of the *erdstalls* was how they broke off into countless tributaries.

"Jean Claude," she called out.

"Here."

Had she heard right?

"Jean Claude," she said again.

"I'm...here"

Ahead. To the right.

She replaced the map in her pocket and headed toward the voice. At an offshoot she aimed the flashlight into the darkness.

"Jean Claude," she called out.

"Here."

Definitely ahead. In the dark.

She moved into the tunnel, which was thick with debris. But she was able to work her way ahead until she came to an obstruction that nearly totally blocked the way. She bent down and shined the flashlight through a small window in the rubble. On the other side she saw Jean Claude. Lying down, struggling to breathe, blood stripping his face and forehead.

"How are you?" she asked.

"My arm's broken."

She studied the obstacle between them. "If that's all we have to deal with, then we're going to be fine."

"You shouldn't be here," he said. "This whole thing could fall in."

She studied the barrier. "How did you get here?"

"I have no...idea. I was watching the tunnel entrance and...the next thing I knew I was out cold and I woke up in here. You need to leave, Mademoiselle Vitt. This is really dangerous."

She ignored his protests and kept examining the rubble. She did not want to go back out then return with the right tools. She decided that a few kicks with her boots might open up enough of a portal to get him out.

But it could also trigger a collapse.

A risk she had to take.

"Can you move back?" she said to him.

She heard him shift his position, groaning in pain.

"Okay," he said. "I'm back."

She sat on the earthen floor and laid the flashlight down. She then pivoted on her butt and slammed both feet into the debris.

Which gave way.

Ever so slightly.

"Sit tight," she said. "I'll have you out shortly."

Chapter Eight

CASSIOPEIA WATCHED AS THE AMBULANCE TOOK JEAN CLAUDE TO THE hospital. She'd extracted him with no problem. The special unit had arrived just as she was exiting the *erdstall*.

"You should not have gone in," the head of the unit said. "There were definitely explosives used here. There could have been more."

She was not in the mood. "I didn't think waiting for you was the smart move. Those tunnels could have collapsed, or Jean Claude might have suffocated."

"I will have to report your recklessness," the man said.

"The last I looked, this is my property, my construction site, so I'll handle things here as I see fit."

She'd always had an independent streak. It was one of the triggers that caused an estrangement with her parents. Luckily, they resolved their differences long before they both died. Sure, she listened and learned and tried to be patient. That was the part of her mother inside her. But when she made a decision, like her father, that was it. And she'd made the decision earlier to handle this herself.

"Report what you want," she told him. "Jean Claude is okay, and that's all that matters."

"A crime has been committed here," one of the police said to her. "It requires investigation."

"I agree, and I plan to do just that."

The police, fire, and special units left. She wasn't a fan of the authorities. More a necessary evil than a true help. That was another thing she and Cotton definitely saw eye to eye on.

She returned to the chateau, while Viktor supervised the cleanup at the construction site.

What did she know for sure?

Esmerelda had been murdered. Her castle had been bombed. Some schoolchildren had violated the *erdstalls*. Someone had attacked Jean Claude, entered the same tunnels and planted explosives, positioning them so they would fell some of the stone walls.

That's it.

And it wasn't much.

The adrenaline rush from earlier was fading, replaced with a familiar fatigue, one that could sap the strength right from her bones.

The *erdstalls* were all over Central Europe, with over 700 in Bavaria alone. Two easily walkable sites were located in Austria and open to the public. But the vast majority were closed off and deemed far too dangerous for people to traverse. Maps existed of them in differing regions. Most were old and antiquated, as there simply was not much interest in the tunnels now. Once they were discovered here on the property, during the foundation work for the castle walls, she'd acquired several medieval maps in an attempt to learn more about them. She'd used a copy of one of those earlier, which had proven relatively accurate. All of them had come from one of her oldest friends.

Nicodème L'Etoile.

He'd been around her entire life, a gnarled, walking stick of a man with a face like the pummeled look of an unfinished sculpture, topped by a mop of unkempt white hair. Probably about eighty-five years old, though she'd never asked him his age. Her father had been an avid collector of rare coins, stamps, and books as well as ancient Egyptian and Roman glass and pottery. Nicodème had long been a dealer in all of those and visited their villa in Spain several times a year, always bringing curiosities for her father's perusal, staying with them, telling stories of the world, then leaving with more money than when he'd arrived. His shop sat in Eze, an ancient mountain village in the south of France. And while he didn't advertise, most rare antique dealers and collectors knew about the storefront, located at #16 on Rue de Barri.

She wondered. Had anyone else bought any old maps? Nicodème could certainly find out. He knew every dealer in the south of France.

She found her cell phone and placed the call. He was #3 on her speed dial, after Cotton and Esmerelda. The older man answered the shop's phone and she explained what had happened, then asked if he could make some inquiries with other dealers and see if anyone had expressed any recent interest in *erdstalls*.

"I don't have to make any inquiries," he told her. "Two weeks ago a man came in without an appointment, which is unusual enough. But this fellow seemed legitimate. He said he was looking for stamps, coins, and maps related to Vienne, Lyon, Givors, and Ambert. I showed him what I had. He asked specifically about *erdstalls*."

That grabbed her attention.

"I only had two maps, both of poor quality. The good stuff you already have, and I mentioned your reconstruction project, which he seemed not to know a thing about. He said he was a dealer, buying for a client who was looking to purchase a home in one of those regions."

"Are your cameras still working?"

After a recent incident in the shop where Nicodème had been attacked, she'd insisted that a security camera be installed to record all visitors. Her old friend had not liked the intrusion on his privacy but had seen the wisdom in the move and allowed it.

"Of course," he said to her. "I promised that I would keep them running and I have."

As she recalled, the system had a thirty-day memory.

"It's not quite noon," she said. "I'm going to find some air travel. I'll be at your shop by six, probably sooner."

"What's this about?" he asked her.

If what was happening was directed at her, and that now seemed logical, Nicodème could be in the crosshairs too.

But no sense unnecessarily alarming him.

"I'll explain when I'm there."

Chapter Nine

TRAVERS SLICED INTO HIS STEAK.

Blood oozed onto the bone china plate, obliterating the ship's monogram etched onto its surface. He liked the outside of his beef well done, but the inside nice and raw. *Black and blue*, was what he called it. And the ship's chef was particularly adept in preparing it exactly that way.

His appetite was that of a man much younger, both in food and women. He was proud of his prowess. No little blue pills needed. Blood infusions for the past decade had him extra healthy, and his daily ritual of calisthenics and swimming in the cold ocean kept him in good shape.

Francesca sat with him at the table under the covered aft deck. She was enjoying one of her green liquid concoctions—the woman rarely ingested solid food—and talking about a fête she wanted to give on the boat for one of her friend's birthdays.

"Would that be okay?" she asked.

He savored another bite. "I prefer for you to rent out some other place. What about the Eden Roc in Cap d'Antibes? It's one of the most exclusive and expensive hotels on the Riviera. Your friend would love that."

"I'm sure my friends would love to see this ship—"

"You aren't supposed to be telling your friends about this place." He pointed with his fork. "Nothing at all. We agreed."

"I haven't given anyone an inventory or spilled any secrets."

That got his attention. "And you know some secrets?"

She tabled her drink. "No. I do not. You need to relax. You've been on edge for weeks, and it seems to be getting worse. What's wrong, Robert?"

He laid his fork down, his appetite fading. "Nothing is wrong. I just don't like strangers on board. This is my sanctuary, and I don't want to share it any more than I want to share you." He hoped a little territorialism would appeal to her. Every woman wanted to feel special. To help make the point he reached over and caressed her cheek. "The Eden Roc. Any weekend you want. Take over the whole place. As many rooms as you need. Cost is irrelevant. All right?"

He watched her calculate the offer. Worth at least half a million, maybe a million.

She wasn't smiling.

Yet.

"And order something from Paris. Couture. Have it made. A one of a kind. Just tell me what color you've chosen and I'll call Van Cleef and have a matching necklace and earrings made."

Now the smile came.

So damn predictable.

"And what would *you* like in return?" she asked.

He could not say the total destruction of Cassiopeia Vitt. But he was well on the way to achieving that. Instead, he appealed to her vanity once again. "How about a repeat performance of last night, tonight?"

She giggled, clearly flattered. "I can do that."

It had actually been quite memorable, especially after the thunderstorm had faded and the sea, along with his anxiety, had calmed. Bedding Francesca seemed excellent therapy. Far more effective and preferable than the nonsense the so-called professionals had recommended.

"Robert, you know you can talk to me," she said. "Anytime about anything. I'm not just here for the presents and parties. I do care about you, and I don't like seeing you so distraught."

He'd heard that before from wives and other women. But he did not require those services from them or Francesca. Not since his mother had any woman occupied such a high spot in his life. Nearly his entire organization was run by men. The ship staffed almost entirely by males. The people he sold arms to and made deals with were primarily men. Women were good for one thing and one thing only.

No sense telling her that, though.

He checked his watch.

"Finish your lunch," he said to her. "I have some matters to deal with in my study. And I look forward to tonight."

He sat at his desk, a bit moved by Francesca's dedication. She was indeed an extraordinary woman who liked to please him in every way. Not clingy. Overly emotional. Or intrusive. But he had no intention of discussing anything with her relative to either his business or his current obsession.

The destruction of Cassiopeia Vitt.

He hated looking back. Forward was all that mattered. But he was clearly standing on a precipice. So far he and his team had managed to stave off total failure with regard to the Repository, but if the press got a hold of any more information, things could take a really bad bounce. He'd already decided that if the fool who was feeding all the sensationalism did not see reason and settle, he'd dispatch others to take care of the problem in a much more permeant way. He'd been hesitant to use force with any of the claimants. First, there were too many. And that would draw attention. Second, he'd thought money would do the trick. Unfortunately, that was not proving to be the case. So violence was coming back on the table. But as far as Cassiopeia Vitt was concerned, violence was the only thing on the table.

He checked his watch. Nearly 5:00 P.M.

He switched on his computer and entered the passcode, which was changed every other day. Within seconds he was watching a scene on the street in a small French town.

Eze.

His man there, Alex Grete, wore a tiny body camera clipped onto his lapel. Grete was walking up an inclined path paved with cobblestones. The image jerked up and down with each step. He caught all of the local flavors. Picturesque buildings with flowering window boxes. Fancifully painted doorways. Shutters. Small shops. And tourists, walking with Grete.

Eze was part town, part museum, a place from another time. Its shops, galleries, hotels, and cafés attracted people by the busload from around the world. The oldest building dated to the early 1300s, the whole thing just a mere few acres and appearing like something created as an amusement park. The tiered village nestled high in the clouds above the French Riviera, about halfway between Nice and Monaco, and carried a mystique. Writers likened it to an eagle's nest atop a rocky seaside peak. He was mindful of the many who'd tried to claim its valuable perch. First the Phoenicians, then Greeks, Romans, Italians, Turks, and Moors. By the 14th century the French had gained a firm hold and the House of Savoy fortified it into a stronghold. From its 430-meter elevation above the sea, an enemy could be seen a day in advance of coming ashore. Its motto was particularly apropos. One he liked.

In death I am reborn.

Eze was also home to someone else near and dear to Cassiopeia Vitt.

Nicodème L'Etoile.

The background information his people had uncovered revealed that the old man's shop sat at the end of one of the village's oldest streets, against the town's outer wall, pressed to the mountain, where not all that many tourists ventured. He never advertised and no signage identified the building or business other than a bronze number 16. The front door stayed locked, and all visits were by appointment only. The display cases inside were filled with rare antique bottles, glasses, bowls, jugs, and jars exhibiting differing styles and craftsmanship from around the world. The shelves were stacked with catalogs and books about glass, pottery, and stone. Vitt's long dead father had been a collector of rare things. Monsieur L'Etoile had done a lot of business with the elder Vitt, enough that the daughter had developed a deep attachment to him.

So the old man in Eze was next.

He watched as Grete found the street and the shop marked 16. An appointment had been made two weeks ago on the pretense of buying antique glass.

The shop seemed as described.

Then something unexpected appeared on the screen.

Cassiopeia Vitt.

Walking ahead of Grete.

She either by coincidence was here, or she'd begun to see a pattern. He was betting on the latter. Interesting. She'd moved faster than he expected. He'd already received a full report on the explosion in Givors. His men had done an admirable job. Grete surely was waiting for instructions. Vitt's presence here, now, was not part of the original plan.

But no matter.

Adapt and change.

That's how he'd always played life.

He reached for the phone and sent a text.

Do This—

And he kept typing.

Chapter Ten

CASSIOPEIA HAD COME TO EZE TO NOT ONLY TAKE A LOOK AT THE security footage, but to also make sure that her old friend was okay. People and things dear to her had already fallen victim. Two additional targets seemed possible. Cotton and Nicodème. One of those two could definitely take care of himself. The other? Not so much. He was an old man who lived a simple, quiet life in an out-of-the-way part of France.

She'd chartered a helicopter at the regional airport near Givors that had flown her directly to an open field not far from Eze. Flying was not something she enjoyed. More a necessary evil. The ride, though, had been smooth and uneventful. She was not sure how long she would stay, but the pilot had told her to take her time. With what she was paying him he could afford to wait.

On arriving, she'd been relieved to discover that everything seemed okay. The shop was functioning, like always, and Nicodème seemed in great spirits. A review of the security footage showed a man of medium height, plain-faced, with short, light brown hair who spoke French with a decisively German accent. Nothing about him seemed threatening. His questions were all intelligent and on point. He seemed to know and understand old maps.

"He was a dealer," Nicodème said to her. "I get a lot of those here. But he wasn't local to Southern France. Which was probably why I did not recognize him."

The appointment had been booked under the name Michel Steinmacher. She immediately tried a few internet searches using the name and came up with nothing. No surprise. It was most likely an alias.

"He bought a few of the old maps," Nicodème said. "None directly on Givors, though."

All of which raised more questions. Was she being led? Sent along a predefined path? If someone had wanted to really do damage at the castle site, the explosives could have been more numerous and more strategically placed. They almost seemed more a warning of some kind.

"Do you still have the maps of Givors?" she asked.

"Of course. I promised them to you. I would never sell them."

He found the maps tucked safely inside their plastic sleeves and laid them on the table. Each was over two hundred years old and in remarkably good condition. She'd studied cartography in college. Maps fascinated her. She had a respectable collection in her chateau, most of which had come from Nicodème. Thankfully, long ago, the various *erdstalls* across the southern part of France had been extensively drawn.

"Can I have your magnifying glass?" she asked.

Nicodème handed her his visor, similar to what jewelers used for precision work. Lightweight magnifying glasses on a leather band, with built-in lights that could be adjusted to shine down on an object. She slipped them on and inspected the map. This one showed the area in and around Givors, where her castle stood, detailing the tunnels beneath. She'd used a copy of another similar map earlier to find Jean Claude.

"When that man from the footage was here, did he take photos of this specific map?"

He shook his head. "I would never allow that."

But that didn't mean he'd not seen what he needed to see, and the guy could have had a terrific memory. Like Cotton. His was eidetic. Not photographic, as the trait was sometimes described, just an extraordinary ability to absorb detail.

She glanced across at the mantle clock.

5:20 P.M.

Her thoughts were interrupted by a knock at the front door.

"My last appointment for the day," he said. "It should not take long, then the two of us can have a lovely dinner."

Nicodème opened the door. "You made excellent time."

The newcomer introduced himself as Paul Froubert, who stated that he'd come to look at some of the antique glass. She noticed that Nicodème did not introduce her, which was fine. No need. The man seemed more interested in the shop's wares and immediately began a perusal. She retreated to the counter and Nicodème joined her.

Monsieur Froubert noticed the maps on the table. "How marvelous. Are these for sale?"

"A few of them are." Nicodème moved closer. "You mentioned glass. I did not know maps were also of interest. Three of these are available at a thousand euros each."

Froubert kept his gaze down at the maps. "That's quite expensive. A bit on the high end."

"They are rare originals."

"Maybe so. But that is way too much. I would be willing to pay half that. Five hundred euros each."

Nicodème smiled. "I do not bargain with my wares. The price is the price."

"Come now, Monsieur L'Etoile," Froubert said. "I buy from dealers like yourself all the time. The markups are unconscionable. Dealers think because they possess certain items they can set the price however they like."

"It is the rarity itself which steers the price."

Froubert shrugged, then leaned forward and studied the maps again. He picked three from the table, handling them more roughly than he should.

"Please be careful," Nicodème said. "They are quite fragile. And one of those you are holding is not for sale."

She saw it was one for Givors that she'd just inspected.

"I am full versed in how to handle antique documents," Froubert made clear.

The tone had changed. More direct. Less friendly.

Borderline rude.

Froubert dropped the maps to the tabletop, seemingly considering things. His right hand reached back into a pocket and returned with a metallic object in view. The hand came up, the arm stiffened, and she heard a hiss.

Then smelled something spicy, acrid.

Nicodème shouted in pain.

Froubert had sprayed an aerosol into the older man's face. Then he was gone. Out the door. With the maps in hand.

She rushed to Nicodème. "Are you okay?"

He nodded. "Pepper spray, I think. Damn thief. Go after him."

She was torn.

But decided that she could catch the guy fast.

So she darted out the door.

She'd run the streets of Eze once before chasing a thief. Now here she was doing it again. The ancient cobblestones were their usual slick, unforgiving selves, and the crowds and twisting path made the effort more difficult. Her target had a thirty-meter head start, moving fast.

Her adrenaline was pumping.

A shopkeeper shouted out, asking if she needed help, but she didn't stop to answer.

The thief rounded a corner.

She caught up and followed.

Ahead was a dead-end street. She raced forward. In front of her rose a two-story stone-front house typical for Eze. Where had he gone? She approached the house and tried the door.

Locked.

Was he inside? Not possible. That would have taken a moment or two to open and close the door, and she would have seen that.

Then she saw it.

A narrow alley between the house before her and the next one, partially concealed by an overgrown bougainvillea vine. She pushed the flowers aside and slipped through, hustling down the narrow passage, barely a half meter wide. At its end she saw the maps lying on the ground within their plastic sleeves. She carefully retrieved them and stared out beyond a waist-high rock wall that guarded the edge of the steep hilltop. Four hundred meters below stretched the Mediterranean Sea. Most of the paths leading down were rocky, overgrown, and dangerous. The drop from the wall to the first bit of solid earth was over ten meters. No way someone jumped that and didn't break a bone. A strong breeze blew in off the sea, the trees swaying to its tune like they were mocking her failure.

She'd lost the thief.

But she had the maps.

She turned to start the walk back to the shop.

A figure stood behind her.

Not Froubert. Someone else.

She heard a hiss.

A spicy scent again filled her nostrils. Her eyes lost focus. She felt a sensation of falling, which accelerated, but she never hit bottom.

As nothingness came fast.

Chapter Eleven

TRAVERS SAID GOODBYE TO FRANCESCA AROUND EIGHT P.M. SHE WAS off to work a runway show in Paris tomorrow, and he'd gifted her with a suite at the Ritz and an American Express card with a one hundred thousand euro credit so she could stay a few days extra and shop. She'd been delighted with both, but he needed her out of the way. He'd been worried about her intrusion into his study during his discussion with Lucian. She most likely heard nothing, but his paranoia, honed from decades of playing both sides against the middle, always screamed caution.

She'd asked if he'd be joining her and he told her no. Paris was not where he liked to spend a lot of time, despite the relative freedom French authorities showed him. And besides, he'd told her, some business associates were arriving for a private meeting. She'd not probed any further, which was another good sign of her ignorance.

He'd stood on the aft deck and watched as the launch, with her aboard, headed for Cannes. They were anchored about twenty kilometers offshore, safely in the no-man's-land of international waters, beyond the reach of any government. The evening was glorious in the fading sunlight, the water dead calm.

No storms today.

He found a pint of Irish whiskey and poured a half-tumbler's measure, then took a seat in one of the deck chairs and waited.

A lot was about to come to a head. He could barely contain his delight. He'd been working toward this moment for the past few months. He'd calmly addressed the problem of the Repository, grasped an understanding of the issues, devised a workable plan, then waited for the opportune moment to implement.

So far, everything had gone perfectly.

He sat for nearly an hour and enjoyed the whiskey, the solitude, and a damp breeze off the ocean. Rarely was he afforded such moments of privacy. He chewed on his thoughts but hated the aftertaste.

Then he heard it.

Faint off the water.

An engine.

Approaching.

He waited in the chair, listening as the sound grew louder. Finally, the skiff appeared from the west and stopped at the floating dock deployed on the ship's starboard side. The sun was gone on the western horizon. He'd told his people to time their arrival after dark.

He stepped over to the starboard railing and stared down.

Two men occupied the skiff.

He'd left orders with the captain that the crew should avoid the dock this evening. His crew were accustomed to making themselves scarce. They were all paid generously for both their performance and discretion. Of course, none of them were fools and understood that they could easily end up at the bottom of the ocean chained to an anchor. So they all did their jobs with no questions asked.

One of the men hopped from the skiff and the other man handed up a black body bag, which was shouldered.

He'd personally designed every room in *Sanctuaire*. The staterooms all had locks, but they worked from the inside. There were storage rooms and other spaces that could be locked with keys, but that would involve the crew way too much.

Only one place would work as a prison.

The music room.

Which came with a heavy-duty steel door and an electronic combination lock. He liked to say the security was there because of the room's many treasures. An ancient Greek flute worth several million euros. Several electric and acoustical guitars, rare collectors' pieces. His Picasso Blue Period Harlequin, one of a kind. And the expensive Matisse seaside landscape and Monet waterlilies. But none of those had belonged to his mother. Her violin, which he'd restored, rested safely in its own sealed, plexiglass case, safe from air and water.

And it was priceless.

He made his way below and arrived at the music room just before the man with the body bag turned the corner. He punched in the code and released the lock, then held the door open.

"On the floor," he said, pointing.

And the man laid the bag down, then left, closing the door behind him.

He stepped over to the ship's phone and connected to the bridge. "Once the skiff is gone, let's get underway at flank speed."

He hung up.

Then bent down and unzipped the bag revealing an unconscious Cassiopeia Vitt.

Now totally under his control.

He'd seized the opportunity and changed the plan, ordering Alex Grete to lead her away from the old man's shop. Originally, he'd planned to kill Nicodème L'Etoile today. But Vitt's appearance caused a change. He could always circle back and kill that old man later.

And he would.

But first things first.

He stared at his quarry.

The soft curve of the chin. An almost innocent roundness in the eyes. Long tangles of thick dark hair hanging past her shoulders. Her body slim and taut, the swarthy skin smooth as satin. Truly stunning. By all reports she was also intelligent, sophisticated, highly-educated, and could handle herself in a tight situation.

A formidable woman of many talents.

She lay with her hands tied behind her back, her ankles bound, and tape across her mouth. His men in Eze had waited until sunset then brought her down from the mount, unnoticed, transporting her to the shore where the skiff had been waiting.

His gaze drifted up past her thighs to her pale-blue shirt. Two of the buttons had come undone and exposed a glimpse of a cream-colored lace brassiere. He admired the swell of her breasts, studying her with the eye of a critic at a work of art.

And he liked what he saw.

Lying before him was the person costing him millions of euros.

Even worse, she'd bested him. Placed his entire reputation in jeopardy. Drawn him into ridicule. Of late, whatever he touched had turned to crap, and no matter how hard he'd tried, he couldn't get the stink off his fingers.

He wanted to destroy her—

More than anything he'd ever wanted in his life.

Chapter Twelve

FRIDAY

CASSIOPEIA RESTED IN THE DEPTHS OF BLACKNESS, A WHIRLPOOL OF light swirling inside her head, growing ever larger, ignoring her subconscious commands to go away.

She opened her eyes.

Her whole body ached, as if she'd been beaten up. When she tried to move, she discovered her hands were tied behind her back, her feet bound, mouth taped.

A touch of fear joined the pain.

Where was she? How had she made it here? The last thing she recalled was standing at the stone wall in Eze. The man behind her. Then something sprayed in her face.

She lay on a hard floor in a room filled with musical instruments displayed inside cases. And a table. With a guitar. That somebody was working on. No windows. Everything elegantly made. What was this place? How long had she been here?

And she was moving.

A soft murmur filled her ears.

A boat?

Yes. She was on a boat.

She grabbed her senses and wiggled across the floor to the door, angling herself so she could kick the steel. Hard. She kept kicking. Sucking air in through her nose, growing more angry by the moment.

The door swung inward, slamming into her boot heels. She rolled back out of the way. A man stood looking down at her.

"Stop it," he spit out. "There's no one to hear you."

She shook her head.

And whined out noise from her taped mouth.

He stepped close, bent down, and pulled back the tape.

"Bathroom," she said.

He spied her carefully, seemingly considering the request. Then he rose and stepped over to a phone on a worktable. He made a call, explained her request to someone, listened a moment, then hung up. He walked back, produced a pocketknife, and cut the tape binding her ankles and wrists. She worked the stiffness from her joints and slowly rose.

Her head cleared.

She walked unsteadily toward the door and out. The man grabbed her roughly by the arm and started to lead her down a corridor.

Enough.

She yanked herself free and drove her right fist into the guy's neck, crushing the larynx and obstructing breathing. He never saw it coming. She brought her right knee into his stomach and doubled him over. She then clenched her hands together and brought them down hard on the nape of the neck, sending the man to the floor.

That felt good.

She located the knife. Not much of a weapon, but better than nothing. She slipped it into her pocket. She had to find out more about where she was, so she headed down the corridor and turned a corner. Standing ten meters away were three men. Two held weapons aimed her way.

The third she recognized.

Robert Travers.

Who stood with his hands clasped behind his back, a sly smile on his lips. "I knew you would make a move. That's why I told him on the phone to cut your bindings. Welcome back. You and I have some unfinished business."

It all made sense in an instant. "You killed Esmerelda?"

He shrugged. "How about you and I retreat into the music room and we can chat."

"Do I have a choice?"

"We always have choices. Yours are just severely limited." He motioned. "Shall we?"

She turned and walked back to the open door, past the guy moaning on the floor. She entered the music room with Travers following. He closed the door. The men with guns were just outside. She walked over and placed the worktable with a guitar atop between her and Travers.

"I had Señora Fontana murdered," he said. "And I bombed your castle."

And she knew why. "To get my attention?"

"Partly. But also so that you can experience some of what I am going through."

She knew from her last encounter with Travers that he loved to wield power. She'd definitely dealt his ego a blow. Big enough for this bastard to kill Esmerelda.

"This is about the Repository? You killed Esmerelda over that?"

"It's about you and me. Nothing more."

She debated kicking his ass right here, right now, and taking her chances with the guys with guns. But this devil had come in here unarmed to confront her for a reason. So like Cotton would say, *Turn on the vacuum cleaner and suck it all in.* "Why am I here instead of being dead too?"

"I want you to see it all."

She heard what was unsaid.

Before I kill you.

"How long was I out?" she asked.

"We kept you under last night and part of today."

So it was Friday. And the boat was moving. Which meant they were no longer in the northern Med, off the coast of France, which had to be where this ship had been waiting. But where were they going?

"I don't suppose you're going to tell me where we are?" she tried.

"Actually, I plan to do just that."

He reached into his pocket and found his cell phone. He tapped the screen and held the unit up.

"*The government of San Marino has an annual summer festival that falls this weekend, and they asked Stephanie to be part of the festivities. She obviously can't, and I couldn't tell her no. So I'm going to fill in on Saturday. The ceremony starts at noon, and I'm told it will be over by one. So I can meet you after that at the Rimini Riviera for some swimming, eating, and other things. You've had a rough week, and I'm guessing you could use a few days of peace."*

Cotton's voice from the call on Wednesday, when they'd made plans for the weekend.

"Intercepting mobile calls is quite easy if you have the expertise, the right equipment, and enough money," he said. "We've been monitoring yours for some time."

This was not good. In a multitude of ways.

"Cotton Malone," he said. "Former intelligence officer for the United States Justice Department, now retired, living in Copenhagen, the owner of a rare bookshop. One with quite a reputation, I might add. I'm going to kill him."

"You might find that more difficult to accomplish than you think."

"True, Malone is definitely an adversary to be careful with. As are you, by the way. But I have the advantage of surprise."

Now she knew why she was here. To ensure she stayed out of the way. Best guess? This ship had rounded the Italian continent and was now somewhere in the Adriatic Sea, headed for the closest point ashore to San Marino, which lay only ten kilometers inland.

He pointed to the LED screen mounted in one corner. "You'll get to watch it all, right here, in the safety and comfort of my music room." He glanced at his watch. "And the big bang is not all that far away. Just a few short hours."

He stepped to the door and opened it. "These men will rebind your wrists and ankles."

The two entered and moved her way.

She felt the power and threat, but also realized that she was not going down without a fight. One of them raised his arm and sprayed more aerosol into her face.

Dammit.

Travers lips stretched back into a gloating grin. "Sleep well."

And the world faded away.

Again.

Chapter Thirteen

SATURDAY

TRAVERS KNEW WHAT IT WAS LIKE TO COVET A PARTICULAR PIECE OF art, crave a certain woman, desire a rare musical instrument, grow his net worth, or long to own the most expensive watch in the world. But he'd not felt this overwhelming, all-consuming desire for satisfaction in a long time.

He may not have been born in the right place, at the right time, but he'd maximized what life had tossed his way. He created a financial empire out of nothing, forging a reputation as a man who could deliver what people wanted. That was exactly why the Repository had worked. Clients felt safe hiding their valuables there under his dutiful care, and he'd enjoyed providing them that security.

He sat in his study.

Cassiopeia Vitt remained bound and gagged below. He'd gassed her yesterday so she'd stay quiet and calm, but she'd awakened by nightfall. There'd been some food and water and two bathroom breaks, both with guns aimed, but there'd been no more trouble. She was now rebound and again unconscious. It was important she stay contained. No interruptions could happen over the next few hours.

The weather for the day seemed perfect. Clear skies. Warm temperatures. Light wind from the north. Today he would kill Cotton Malone and Nicodème L'Etoile. Tomorrow, Cassiopeia Vitt.

Or maybe even later today, depending how he felt.

"Everything is ready," Lucian said, entering the room.

They'd traveled a long way fast, speeding from the Ligurian Sea off the French coast, around the boot of Italy, and up into the Adriatic, now anchored in international waters off the coast of Italy. It would have been quicker to just stay on the east side of Italy and drive across to San Marino. But that would have entailed three hours in a car, with *Sanctuaire* too far away. He had to be prepared for any hasty escape. Now he was just a short boat ride from shore, San Marino equally close. Any trouble and he could flee west across the Adriatic to Montenegro or Croatia, which had always offered him safe haven.

"The car is waiting?" he asked.

Lucian nodded. "And everything else is ready at the site."

He'd caught a break with the San Marino government scheduling the appreciation ceremony to coincide with their annual Medieval Days Festival. Thousands of people would be within the city's ancient walls for a three-day celebration. Their research indicated that the cobbled streets would rumble with the sound of drums as the crowds followed bands and bagpipes. There would also be lots of ritual and tradition in reenactments that included costumed parades, courtly games, falconry, and sipping on mead. Most of the attendees would be costumed, which would allow them easy access in and out unnoticed.

"What time is the parade?" he asked Lucian.

"Eleven A.M. And they're noted for their punctuality."

Perfect.

Although a separate country, surrounded by Italy on all sides, there were no border controls into or out of San Marino. That meant easy access, with thousands of revelers for cover.

"Malone stayed last night at a local inn in old town, an easy walk from there to the ceremony," Lucian said. "We should be able to follow him from our high location."

He checked his watch.

10:00 A.M.

Time to move.

Lucian motioned to the map of the City of San Marino lying on the desk, one of those that had arrived by e-mail which he'd printed out. It showed the tiny sliver of the old town enclave that stretched out along Mount Titano. Stone walls enclosed everything, the roads inside closed to traffic. The main route, Piazza della Libertà, was lined with cafés, restaurants, and shops, all of which would be doing brisk business.

Duty-free shopping was one of the town's attractions to visiting Italian tourists. Three fortresses stood above the town, linked by a stone path that ran along the mountain ridge.

Lucian lifted a pen and placed an X above a building at the northwest wall. "That's the Basilica di San Marino. The ceremony will take place on the stone steps out front. There's a small piazza there which should be full of people."

He scanned the map.

And saw his vantage point.

The oldest of the three fortresses, which crowned the long ridge of Mount Titano, was Rocca Guaita, constructed in the 11th century. Steep stone steps wound a path up to it from the city, where panoramic views of the surrounding countryside were offered. That same lofty perch provided an unobstructed view of the Basilica di San Marino.

Where Travers would be shortly.

Lucian circled the fortress. "We walk in costumed. Part of the festivities. We should be able to walk out the same way. The confusion we'll create will offer the perfect cover."

He agreed. "And the cell phone towers?"

"They'll be incapacitated around eleven thirty."

The idea was to isolate the tiny republic, add to its troubles, and also provide them with a cleaner path of escape.

Which was needed.

He'd opted to handle this task himself. Lucian had been practicing and was ready to go. Together they would kill Cotton Malone, recording it all for Cassiopeia Vitt to see once they returned to the ship. The old man in Eze would be next. Which she'd be forced to watch too.

Then she would die.

Slowly.

After that, he'd deal with the remaining lawsuits in a more unconventional way. One he'd found always effective. Money had not worked.

But violence never failed.

Chapter Fourteen

CASSIOPEIA WOKE FOR THE THIRD TIME.

Her head seemed trapped in a fog, but she quickly shook off the effects of the aerosol and focused on her situation. Her wrists and ankles were rebound with tape, her mouth sealed too. Enough of this. Travers was planning on killing Cotton and Nicodème. Anyone else and she might mistake all that for bravado. But Travers was a narcissistic psychopath fully capable of carrying out his threats. He'd tried to kill her months ago and failed. Then he disappeared. Now he was back. And she was lying on the floor amongst a collection of musical instruments. Helpless? Possibly, and that bothered her.

Rope had some give. She could work it loose. But tape? That was tough. She moved her legs and arms to try and expand the bindings.

Nothing.

She recalled the room. The table beside her was loaded with tools. But they were all a meter high and out of reach. Could she topple the table to get to what's on it? No. The legs were bolted to the floor.

Another bathroom break?

She doubted that was going to work either.

Way too many guns.

The two men dearest to her in the world were in trouble.

She had to get to them.

The door opened, then closed.

She wiggled her body around, ready to face the guard who entered. But it wasn't a man.

"Robert Travers knows me as Francesca," the woman said in English. "But my name is Anneke Koremans."

The woman was young, thin, with short blonde hair, dressed in some outrageously expensive clothes. Francesca crouched down and removed the tape from her mouth.

"I'm with *Direction Générale de la Sécurité Extérieure.*"

The DGSE. Equivalent to Britain's MI6 and the American CIA. The French national security service, there to gather intelligence and conduct paramilitary and counterintelligence operations. It also dealt with economic espionage. She'd visited its headquarters in the 20th arrondissement of Paris several times.

"I've been working this assignment for a while now," Francesca said. "Travers has an eye for women of a certain look and type. I was dangled as bait, and he took it."

Francesca removed the tape from Cassiopeia's wrists and ankles.

"With the help of some modeling agencies and a few of the couture houses, I established myself as a high-priced model," Anneke said. "But the time has come to end the charade."

She noticed that the woman was speaking low, almost in a whisper.

"How did you get in here?" she asked.

"Travers thinks I'm in Paris. He dropped me ashore yesterday. He made sure I was gone before you were brought aboard."

She worked out the stiffness in her hands and feet. "How long?"

"What?"

"How long have you been with Travers?"

"Months. I arrived shortly before you brought down the Repository."

"He murdered Esmerelda Fortuna. And you just let him?"

"I had no idea that happened until after."

But she was not convinced.

"Look," Anneke said, "Travers is fully versed in how to stay out of reach. But, finally, thanks to you, we have him where we want him."

She realized this woman was right. Taking down someone like Travers would not be easy. And they would only get one shot. So it had to be a kill shot.

"What are you doing here?" she asked the woman.

"I came back for you. Thankfully, I have the run of the ship, and no one questioned my arrival."

"Are you here alone? No backup?"

"For the moment. I flew from Nice to Rome, then drove to the coast. I waited for Travers to leave, then came out here by boat. I come and go all the time. Nothing unusual about it."

"Travers is planning on killing an ex-American agent named Cotton Malone. He's in San Marino today for a ceremony. He's also going after a man who lives in Eze. Nicodème L'Etoile. He has to be warned and protected."

"To do that, we'll need to leave the ship."

"All we need is a cell phone."

"No one is allowed to have one on board except for Travers."

Made sense. "Then let's get out of here."

"Let me deal with the guard," Anneke said.

"How did you even get in here?"

"I told them that Travers asked me to speak with you. Like I said, they don't question me."

But they might now.

Anneke approached the door and motioned for Cassiopeia to stay to one side, out of sight, then she turned the latch. Cassiopeia decided that the chances of talking their way out of here was, as Cotton would say, *slim to none*. And, besides, she was in a foul mood. Being drugged and kidnapped did that to her. Travers was out there, free, headed for San Marino, with Cotton in his sights.

So she stepped into the doorway and caught the surprised look in the guard's eyes. With no hesitation she drove her fist into his jaw, then kicked him across the narrow corridor. The back of his head slammed hard into the solid wall, stunning him. She made sure he stayed down with a solid kick to the face.

Blood oozed from the nose.

She relieved him of his gun.

"Apparently, you know how to handle yourself," Anneke said.

"Don't worry about me."

And she meant it.

She dragged the downed guard into the music room and bound his hands and feet with the tape from the worktable, then she slapped a piece across his mouth. They left and headed toward the upper decks, careful with their steps. So far they'd seen no one. She had no idea how they would get off the ship. Perhaps in the same boat Anneke had used to get here. There had to be quite a few crew on a ship this size, but they all couldn't be involved with Travers' activities. That would be far too many eyes and ears to keep quiet.

"Where are we going?" she whispered to Anneke, who seemed intent on heading somewhere.

"Travers' study. It needs searching before we leave."

She was more concerned about Cotton and getting word to him, but understood the wisdom of what Anneke was saying.

To get Travers she needed evidence.

They were headed toward the front of the ship, down a long corridor lined with closed doors. Anneke stopped at a double set. She opened one of the panels and they entered what was Travers' shipboard office. A large room with sleek furniture and an awesome view out the windows past the ship's bow with its helicopter landing pad.

Anneke locked the doors from the inside and began a search. Cassiopeia watched, but something on the desk caught her attention. A map of San Marino. She bent down close and noticed two markings. An X and another site circled.

"This is where he's headed," she said.

Anneke stopped searching and studied the map too.

"He told me that he was going to kill Cotton." She pointed. "That's where Cotton is right now. Is there anyone out there supporting you as backup?"

Anneke shook her head. "We didn't want to risk spooking Travers. So it's just me. I came across Italy alone to get you out of here."

Which she appreciated. "Let's get to shore. Where's the boat you came in?"

"Tied to the floating dock on the starboard side."

She heard a low, distant rumble. She stepped toward the forward windows and stared out at the sunny day. The rhythmic beating of a helicopter's engine grew louder. Off the port bow a small chopper swung in from the west, hovered, then landed on the elevated pad. The blades wound down and the pilot exited the cabin.

"Too bad we can't fly that thing," Cassiopeia said. "We need the speed."

"Who says we can't?"

She caught the smile on the woman's thin lips.

"I flew helicopters in the French army."

Chapter Fifteen

TRAVERS WALKED THE STREETS OF SAN MARINO. HE WAS DRESSED AS A medieval nobleman in a colorful costume that he'd had made special for today. Lucian was likewise decked out as a squire, which included a backpack where the tools they would soon need could be easily concealed. Many others were likewise festively attired.

San Marino had been founded by a saint, then forged through conflict. It now carried the title of the last remaining feudal state, possessed of a fiercely independent streak, one he could readily identify with. The festival was designed to celebrate that independence. Three castle ruins rose from the mountain ridge overhead, standing guard. The oldest, Guaita, dated to the 11th century and had once been a prison. The second, Cesta, rose from the highest summit of Monte Titano, built in the 13th century, now housing a museum containing thousands of ancient weapons. The smallest, the 14th century Montale, worked double duty as a prison and fort. Now they were all tourist attractions, their connecting ramparts opened to all and boldly decorated for the celebration.

He checked his watch.

11:25 A.M.

He stared up at Rocco Guaita and the inclined path leading to the fortress. People were climbing toward the ancient route. He and Lucian purposefully avoided the area around the basilica so as not to come onto anyone's radar. With the local governmental authorities present, security would be focused there. The repatriation ceremony for the Domagnano

Treasure would start at noon. On the podium would be the captains regent, the two elected every six months by the country's legislative body, usually from opposing parties, vested with executive power over the republic. That odd tradition dated back to 1243. Members of the Grand and General Council would also be present, as would the judiciary. Plenty of dignitaries to die with Cotton Malone.

The question remained whether anyone would care. Though a member of the United Nations, San Marino was not part of the European Union. More a thorn in Italy's side, he wondered if any tears would be shed for its fallen leaders. Certainly no one would care about Malone. He was a former Justice Department operative who'd retired out a few years ago. Insignificant. Irrelevant. He doubted that anyone would even associate the attack with him. After all, he was merely filling in for his ex-boss, Stephanie Nelle. More than likely the investigation would focus on San Marino and its peculiar blend of politics.

"Let us head up to the Guaita," he said to Lucian.

A colorful costumed parade was making its way through the narrow streets. Music blared from speakers. Drummers led the way. Excited people lined the edges. They slipped past the crowd and found the stone stairs leading upward toward the mountain ridge and the three fortresses. The climb worked his calves and strained his breathing. But he was in good physical shape and could handle the exertion.

The day was spectacular. Bright azure sky. Not a cloud in sight. A summer sun overhead. Being seven hundred and fifty meters high helped moderate the temperatures, keeping them around twenty Celsius, and making it not uncomfortable to be costumed.

San Marino's military forces were among the smallest in the world. It was dependent on Italy for its national defense. But there were some local militias that performed ceremonial duties, patrolled borders, guarded government buildings, and assisted police in major criminal cases. Like the one he was about to generate.

The Guard of the Rock was the frontline military unit, and he'd already seen a dozen decked out in their red and green uniforms. The Guard of Nobles, in their more striking blue, white, and gold uniforms were also out in abundance. They were charged with protecting the captains regent and defending the Grand and General Council. Several of them should be on or near the stage during the repatriation ceremony. The rest of the local security forces were not a problem.

The Company of Uniformed Militia was, on paper, the basic fighting force of San Marino, but it was largely ceremonial. They paraded around in dark blue uniforms, with a kepi bearing a blue and white plume. The Gendarmerie were more like police, protecting citizens and property and preserving law and order. But they'd never experienced anything like what was about to happen.

They made it to the top and stared across the sharp fall of the valley to other distant peaks. The countryside for kilometers in every direction could be clearly seen.

"Quite a perch," he muttered.

They moved toward the inner parapets that faced the city itself. Below was the Basilica di San Marino. A neoclassical building from the early 19th century, built on the foundations of a 4th century Romanesque church. Dedicated to St. Marinus, who founded the city. He'd read about its interior. A classic style with a long nave and two side aisles lined with seven altars adorned with statuary and paintings. An urn at the high altar contained the relics of St. Marinus himself. The Piazza Domus Plebis stretched out in front, down nine steps from the main doors. Not a large piazza, enough room for a couple of hundred spectators. A podium and chairs had been placed at the top of the wide stairs, ready for the ceremony. He imagined the dignitaries, including Cotton Malone, were inside the church, awaiting the strike of noon.

Lucian slipped off his shoulder pack and removed the electronic controller, positioning it on the stone wall between two of the parapets that faced away from the city, toward the countryside. They both crowded close to shield it from view. Thankfully, few people were up this high as yet. Most of the visitors filled the streets below, enjoying the festivities.

He found the walkie-talkie in his pocket and depressed the talk button. "We are here."

Sixty seconds later a voice said, "Done."

That meant the drone was now airborne. Two hired operatives were stationed about a half kilometer away in a straight sight line from their perch. The Firefly was a proven workhorse, made of high-grade carbon fiber with an aluminum frame. Designed for the toughest weather conditions. Able to carry a payload of up to twenty kilograms. This one was loaded with fifteen kilograms of high explosive. It would approach from the north, and their height would allow them to shortly assume its command. For now, it was being controlled by the men who'd sent it aloft.

Lucian's hands dropped to the controller and he readied himself.

"On the way," was the next transmission.

He kept his eyes peeled to the north. Drones were tough to spot. But they'd practiced enough with this one to know when to hand off electronic control.

A green light appeared on the controller.

Signal acquired.

Altitude, speed, and range displays came to life.

"I have her," Lucian said.

Then he spotted the drone.

Speeding toward them.

Still out over the countryside, but rapidly making its way toward the City of San Marino.

Chapter Sixteen

CASSIOPEIA DID NOT ARGUE WITH GOOD FORTUNE, SHE MERELY silently thanked the foresight of whoever inside French intelligence had decided that their plant with Robert Travers should be able to fly a helicopter.

Finally, a break.

They'd gathered the map from Travers' desk, then made their way out toward the ship's bow. The chopper sat quiet on the pad. The day was bright and sunny. Not a speck of wind. The water a dead calm.

"Once you start the rotor we're going to have company," she said. "Some of whom might have guns."

"Then it's a good thing you have one too. Just keep them back long enough for us to get out of here."

No problem.

They hustled out the door and into the sun.

Ten meters across the foredeck and they were on the landing pad and into the helicopter. The aircraft appeared lightweight, which should offer speed and maneuverability. The flight deck was all glass, with plenty of LED screens. Seats accommodated four passengers. Anneke wasted no time and started tapping the screens and activating switches.

"Here we go," she said.

And the blades began to turn as the rotor wound up.

Faster. Faster.

Two men rushed out onto the foredeck and headed their way. The rotors leveled off at full thrust. Anneke worked the pedals and cyclic, lifting them off the pad just as the men arrived. The chopper banked right, then powered off into the sky, headed west, toward shore.

"You know where we are?" she asked Anneke.

"San Marino is twenty kilometers dead ahead. We'll be there in a few minutes."

She hated flying. And this was her second helicopter in two days. But Cotton needed her, so phobias be damned. She felt angry and frustrated. Esmerelda had been murdered for no reason other than revenge. How would she ever come to terms with that? And Nicodème? He was now in the cross hairs too. But she flushed all that anxiety from her brain and focused.

One thought was clear.

If the opportunity presented itself, she would end Robert Travers.

"Do you have any idea what he's planning?" she asked Anneke.

"I'm afraid I don't. One of the crew told me about you being brought to the ship. You were the one who ended the Repository and caused Travers so much grief, so I assumed he planned to kill you. That's why I came back."

"He wanted me to first watch while he killed my boyfriend, Cotton Malone, then another dear friend who lives in Eze."

"He enjoys being in charge."

She did not want to ask what this woman had been forced to endure in order to ingratiate herself with a psychopath like Travers.

But none of it could have been good.

They passed the shoreline, with its white sandy beaches lapped by the blue Adriatic. Then a town with a collection of whitewashed houses and narrow streets tumbling down toward the water. Somewhere down there she and Cotton would have spent the weekend.

What a lovely thought.

Anneke kept the chopper powering forward through the clear skies. The landscape miniaturized with their increasing altitude. The topography began to change with a mixture of highlands and valleys. The Apennine mountain range loomed ahead, which stretched the length of the Italian peninsula. Forests thickened below, the clear valleys home to farms and villages. Roads crisscrossed in all directions. A brassy sun added welcome definition to it all.

She checked her watch.

12:05 P.M.

The ceremony starts at noon, and I'm told it will be over by one. So I can meet you after that at the Rimini Riviera for some swimming, eating, and other things.

Whatever Cotton was doing had already started.

Ahead she spotted Monte Titano. The highest point for kilometers in every direction. About seven hundred and fifty meters. The views from there stretched northwest to the Apennines and east to the coast. She knew on a clear day you could actually see across the Adriatic to the Dalmatian coast. The long, slender stretch of the City of San Marino angled up the slopes. Three castles punctuated the mountain's long ridge, rising to the highest, Rocca Cesta. They were linked by a paved path, the Passo delle Streghe, Witches' Passage. She and her parents had walked it many times. The iconic three towers were shown on both the San Marino flag and coat of arms, the whole place now a UNESCO World Heritage Site.

She smiled.

Cotton had a bad history with those, however unintentional.

She found the map they'd taken from Travers' desk and located the point that had been circled. Rocca Guaita. To the left of Cesta.

"I'm going to assume that this circle is there for a reason," she said to Anneke. "Head for the middle fortress."

Anneke banked, then straightened their course.

People were coming into view inside the walled enclave.

The Guaita consisted of a central fortress tower and two rings of walls, the outer ring adorned with battlements. She knew from prior visits that its defensive fortifications were vital in the 15th century, when San Marino was at war with a nearby Italian noble family. She searched the walkways. A few people were milling back and forth, many in costume. Many more were parked at the wall, watching what was happening below in the city. Her gaze drifted away from the tower and into the city. She spotted a crowd gathered before the basilica. What had been marked with an X on the map. A speaker was standing at the podium addressing them.

Then she saw Cotton.

Standing in a line of people behind the podium, listening to the person speaking.

"The ceremony has started," she said to Anneke. "Swing back around to the Guaita."

The chopper circled back closer to the tower. Two costumed

figures caught her attention, standing at the wall between the parapets. Their attention out over the countryside that stretched for kilometers below them. Everybody else was focused on the festival. But not these two.

She pointed. "There. Let's get closer."

Anneke manipulated the cyclic and brought the helicopter down closer. The two figures, one wearing some sort of medieval nobleman's attire, the other as a peasant or squire, glanced up. Both were masked, but she immediately recognized the taller one.

Travers.

What were they doing?

The shorter man's two hands were working something.

"That's a drone controller," she said to Anneke.

And her gaze shot out to the sky ahead. Searching.

Looking.

Left. Right.

Ahead.

Chapter Seventeen

TRAVERS HAD RECONNOITERED SAN MARINO IN EVERY DETAIL. HIS
minions had provided drawings and photographs of all the key locations.
The maps that had come by e-mail completed the information needed.
He was taking a chance coming here, overseeing this killing himself. But
it was important that Cassiopeia Vitt know that it had been him who'd
killed the love of her life. He'd worked through all of the details,
imagining the walk up to the tower, the scurry away after the drone had
done its damage, the trek out of the city and back to their car. Another
team had already reported that the cell phone towers servicing the city
had been disabled, isolating the area. Sure, they'd be repaired, or the
signals rerouted, but that would take time. More than enough of a delay
for them to compete this task.

"Where is the drone?" he asked.

"A thousand meters out, coming this way," Lucian told him.

Then he heard a new sound. A bit unexpected. The thump of a
helicopter. A VIP visitor coming to the festival? Possibly. He turned
and stared past the elevated walkway, between the parapets, out over the
city to the sky beyond. He spotted the aircraft coming straight in.

Then it hit him.

That was *his* helicopter. The one kept stored on the ship, used for
longer forays from open water to shore, brought out this morning and
readied for use if needed. His pilot had been told to make a test flight
and ensure all was functioning, then wait on the ship. He did not want
to use such a conspicuous means of escape, but would if necessary to

make his way back to open water where the laws were much more fluid.

With its heavy payload, the drone had a flight time of around fifteen minutes before its batteries were exhausted. Lucian had activated a timer once he'd acquired the signal. A quick glance at the electronic display showed they had nine minutes left.

More than enough.

But the helicopter.

What was it doing here?

Its presence in the sky could compromise everything.

Unfortunately, the disabling of the cell towers worked both ways. He had no way of connecting with the ship to determine why the chopper had flown inland. That was not part of the plan. Of course, no one on the ship had any idea what he was doing here. That information was for Lucian only.

"How far?" he asked, still watching the helicopter.

"Four minutes."

The helicopter clattered overhead, turning and twisting, swinging around and surveying Guaita. The sun was bright and reflective off the chopper's windscreens, making it difficult to see who was inside. But it had definitely swooped in and flown straight here. Troubling, since no one on the ship knew he and Lucian would be at this precise point within the ancient city.

He moved away from Lucian and crossed the stone walkway to the inner side of the Witches' Walk. Below, he saw street performers, trumpeters, bag pipe players, coin makers, weavers, and potters. In one of the squares drummers and dancers performed. He noticed flag wavers and a man practicing falconry. In other parts vendors sold mead and various foodstuffs. A crossbow tournament was in progress, and people had lined up for the archery contest. The ceremony before the basilica seemed in full swing. The distance made hearing the speaker impossible.

But he saw Cotton Malone. Recognized him from the photographs he'd been provided. Stepping to the podium.

The chopper was powering around.

He stepped back to Lucian.

And saw the drone out in the bright azure sky. Silently approaching, about two hundred meters up.

"He's speaking," he told Lucian.

CASSIOPEIA SPOTTED A DRONE IN THE AIR.

Out in the open sky beyond the walls.

Heading toward the city.

Carrying a payload.

And the big bang is not all that far away. Just a few short hours.

That's what Travers had said back on the ship when he'd thought her no threat.

"That has to be explosives," she said.

Anneke had halted the helicopter's advance, hovering over the city.

Think. Now. Fast.

"Go to it," she said.

Anneke tossed her a quizzical glance. Like, *are you serious.*

"Do it," she ordered.

Anneke engaged the cyclic. The blades bit into the air and drove them forward. They could not collide with the drone. That would be suicide. The gun from the ship was tucked at her waist, but using it would require some amazing shots with perfect aim. And they'd have to get way too close. The resulting explosion could bring them down. The one thing she could not allow, though, was the drone to make it to the city walls.

An idea occurred to her.

She searched the cockpit and spotted three folded towels on the two rear seats. The top one bore the stitched outline of the *Sanctuaire.* She reached back and retrieved all three.

"Get us close and right above it," she said.

Anneke seemed to understand exactly what she had in mind and worked the flight controls, synching the cyclic with the peddles and easing back on the throttle. They quickly overtook the drone, then Anneke swung them back around and brought them just above the threat. Cassiopeia estimated they were less than five hundred meters from the city walls. Obviously, Travers intended on flying the drone right into the ceremony where Cotton was present. Drones were quick, quiet, and clever. But also vulnerable.

She released the hatch.

"You're going to have to get real close," she said over the wind roar.

Anneke nodded and dropped their altitude a few meters. The drone was now right outside.

"Ahead, past it some," she yelled.

Anneke maneuvered the chopper just beyond the drone, which now flew about a meter below and behind the landing struts.

Three chances.

She balled up one of the towels and, forcing the hatch open against the forward draft, she tossed it out ahead of the drone. The cloth immediately unfolded and swept back, just above the four spinning blades, rushing away.

A miss.

She quickly balled the next towel and tried again.

Another miss.

TRAVERS WATCHED IN HORROR AS *HIS* HELICOPTER INTERCEPTED THE drone, and someone was tossing towels out to try and take it down. The midday sun kept a glare on the windscreen, but as the chopper kept shifting position he managed to get a look inside the cabin.

Two passengers.

Cassiopeia Vitt in the passenger's seat.

Francesca behind the controls.

What?

How was any of that possible?

CASSIOPEIA STARED AHEAD.

They were racing toward the city.

The walls coming up below them fast.

"Do it again," Anneke said, "and let me see if I can help you."

She readied the towel, eased the hatch open, and tossed it down. At the instant before she released her grip, Anneke dipped the chopper, bringing it even closer. The towel unfolded in the midday air and swept back, engulfing the four high-speed revolving blades like a shroud. They tore into the terrycloth, shredding some. The towel wreaked its damage, obstructing the blades, causing the drone to falter, its altitude and speed affected, the carriage rocking side to side.

Bits of the blades shattered off.

Then more.

The drone lost its lift.

TRAVERS COULD NOT BELIEVE WHAT HE WAS SEEING.

But the course was clear.

"Detonate it," he said. "Now."

And Lucian pushed the button.

CASSIOPEIA'S ATTENTION SHOT FROM THE FALLING DRONE TO THE walls, where Travers still stood.

They were nearly there.

"Veer off. Fast," she yelled.

Anneke worked the pedals and jerked them into a hard left turn.

Just as the drone exploded.

Chapter Eighteen

TRAVERS WANTED THE HELICOPTER DESTROYED, BUT ITS BANKING, combined with the drone dropping fast from the sky, had moved it out of harm's way. The explosion flashed in an expected burst of light, the drone shattering into fragments flying in all directions, a fireball emerging outward from the center. A second explosion blotted the first from view. If all had gone well, that one would have finished the job the first had started. But now, thanks to gravity and Vitt's ingenuity, none of that would happen.

Dammit.

Malone was now beyond his reach and Cassiopeia Vitt was free. Not to mention Francesca. Piloting the helicopter?

But first things first.

"We need to leave," he said to Lucian.

The younger man nodded and stuffed the controller back into the backpack, which Lucian slipped onto his shoulders. The helicopter was still out over the countryside, regaining altitude, climbing back up the slopes of Mount Titano. He and Lucian hustled down the Witches' Walk, high over the city, in a casual pace, trying not to draw attention to themselves.

Thoughts swirled through his brain.

What if Vitt had alerted the authorities? She'd obviously figured out what he'd planned. Yes. He'd taunted her with what was to come, but he'd not really given her much thought considering the last time he saw her she was bound, gagged, and unconscious in the music room.

But Francesca?

Who the hell was she?

He always vetted the women he spent more than one night with. Sometimes even the one-night stands were given a cursory look. Francesca, because of her longevity and access to the ship, had been carefully investigated. Everything had checked out. She was a high-priced runway model, employed by a top-notch French agency.

Nothing had flagged.

But apparently it had all been a ruse.

She was definitely something else.

CASSIOPEIA WAS IMPRESSED AS ANNEKE HANDLED THE CONTROLS AND kept the chopper in the air, despite the explosion. Gauges fluctuated. The rotors coughed. The aircraft bucked like a donkey, but eventually settled down. She searched the ramparts and spotted Travers making his escape. Beyond the walls, down in the city, people seemed oblivious to what just happened. Surely, they'd heard the explosion, but they could have thought it all part of the festival.

Travers and the other guy kept moving.

The bastard was trying to destroy her life. No way. Not going to happen. Cotton was safe. Nicodème? Hard to say. But she would deal with the threat to him as soon as she cut the head from the snake. A fissure of anxiety swept through her, but an overwhelming anger overcame any fear.

She cautioned herself.

That had to be controlled.

Anger caused mistakes.

"The one in the squire costume is Lucian," Anneke said. "He's Travers' right hand and never far away. Whatever Travers does, Lucian does too."

Good to know.

"Get me down to the walkway," she told Anneke.

The chopper descended, but there was little room to land.

"As close as you can and I'll jump."

Anneke maneuvered to about a meter above the stone. Few people were there, and the ones that were stayed back out of the way. Cassiopeia opened the hatch, stepped onto the landing strut, then leaped off.

Anneke quickly climbed away.

And the wash of the blades faded with her.

TRAVERS HEARD THE HELICOPTER AND TURNED BACK TO SEE Cassiopeia Vitt hit solid stone, on her feet, running his way. His escape options were now limited. No way to contact the ship. No way to contact anyone. Not until they were away from San Marino and headed back toward the coast. Their car was parked below the city in a roped-off field, with all of the other visitors' transportation. They'd blended right in. He'd intended on doing the same after the drone had struck. But Vitt's appearance had changed everything. Never had he experienced this level of blind terror. Always he'd been in control. But his heart thumped with a massive resonance and sweat poured from him. He needed options. And decided the Cesta might offer a way to gain an advantage. The 13th century palace housed the Museum of Historical Weapons. If nothing else, he might find something to defend himself with.

He turned onto another path and quickly climbed toward the fortress.

A quick glance back confirmed that Vitt was following.

CASSIOPEIA WATCHED AS HER TARGETS, A HUNDRED METERS AWAY, turned and were now headed up toward the Cesta fortress. She knew about the place. Home to over 1,500 displayed weapons, armors, and devices from the Middle Ages to the beginning of the 19th century. Thankfully, few people were up this way, the vast majority of visitors down below in the city enjoying the festivities. The gun remained tucked at her waist beneath her exposed shirttail, ready for use.

Her entrance on the scene had surely attracted the attention of security personnel below. A helicopter swooping down close and a person leaping from it would require immediate investigation. So she had to assume the local authorities were headed up this way. She really did not require their assistance since arresting Robert Travers was not part of her plan.

But was murder?

Even for someone so deserving?

That was not a line she'd ever crossed. Sure she'd defended herself, but never had she been the aggressor.

Would she be today?

TRAVERS, WITH LUCIAN IN TOW, ENTERED THE MUSEUM, BYPASSING THE admissions window. The attendant called out in Italian for them to stop, but he ignored the guy.

The first hall they found was mostly cut and thrust weapons. Lots of partisans, scythes, halberds, and spears hanging from the walls. Across the corridor, in another room, he saw armor, olden firearms, and knives.

He pointed. "Get a few of those."

Lucian moved to the wall, retrieved four of the knives from their holders, and handed him two of the blades. He was annoyed by the tenseness in the younger man's face.

"Get a grip," he ordered.

Lucian nodded. "Francesca was flying that helicopter."

"I know. We'll deal with her once we're away from here."

He realized that Vitt would arrive momentarily. His gaze scanned the compact hall and he counted two other exits out to, he supposed, more viewing halls.

He pointed.

"We need to trap her. That way. Let's go."

CASSIOPEIA ENTERED THE BUILDING.

A man waited for her outside the admissions window who explained that two men had barged inside without paying. She told him to leave, but she wanted to know if there were any other visitors inside. The man shook his head and told her in Italian that the museum had just opened at noon.

"Go get the police," she said, keeping to Italian. "And lock the door on your way out."

He hesitated, seemingly unsure of what to do. She reached to her waist and found the gun. His eyes went wide, and he quickly scurried toward the main entrance. One more thing.

"Are there cameras back there?"

The man called out *no* as he left, and she heard the lock engage.

Time to find the bastard.

A clammy, tight band of fear encircled her chest like a snake. Her usual tidy mind swirled in turmoil. But all that worked to sharpen her senses and steel her nerve. For Esmerelda, she told herself.

Cautiously, she entered the first room, crammed with weapons. But no one was there. She moved through and entered the next one. Still, no one in sight. They were both here. She knew it, and they knew she was here too.

Travers was drawing her in.

No question.

It's never good to be the fox in the hunt, Cotton liked to say. *But the fox does have one advantage. He's out front.*

Which provided room to move in any direction.

Just don't be predictable.

TRAVERS FINALLY FOUND WHAT HE'D BEEN LOOKING FOR.

An exit outside.

It opened out from the far end of the last viewing hall, the largest of the five in the building, this one displaying submachine guns, revolvers, muskets, and more swords. The locals were surely headed this way. But he needed time to both kill Vitt and make his escape.

He faced Lucian. "I want you to take a position over there," and he pointed, "between those two display cases. I'll be here. Vitt has to come here. When she does, I'll draw her in and you kill her."

They both held two knives each.

Lucian did not appear to be on board with his plan, so he said, "I assure you, if you don't kill her she will kill us."

That got the younger man's attention.

And a nod indicated that he understood.

CASSIOPEIA PASSED THROUGH ANOTHER GROUP OF DISPLAYS, THIS ONE A mixture of grenade launchers, more machine guns, and assault rifles. Lots of military uniforms too.

"I am in here."

Travers' voice. In English.

From the next room.

She stepped to the open doorway, the gun leading the way. Travers stood across the hall amidst an array of more weapons. He held two large knives in his outstretched hands. She doubted this bastard had ever been in a tight spot like this. Travers was the type who hired others to do his dirty work, staying in the shadows, off to the side, out of the line of fire. But not this time. He was right in the cross hairs. Literally. She stared him down past the gun's sight.

But where was Lucian?

He's Travers' right hand and never far away.

She caught movement out of the corner of her eye and wheeled.

Lucian.

Advancing with two knives of his own.

She sent a bullet Travers' way, then launched herself at her assailant, kicking one of the blades from his grasp. Her move seemed to catch Lucian totally off guard. Then she realized, this guy had never been in a fight.

The weapon tumbled to the floor.

With her free hand she grabbed his arm and yanked Lucian forward, tripping his legs out from under him in an attempt to send the man down face first to the floor. But Lucian was big and solid and managed to regain his balance, steading himself, replanting his feet, and facing her, still holding one of the knives. Her gaze shot past him to Travers, who had dodged the bullet and now gripped one of the knives by the tips of his fingers. His arm cocked back, ready to launch the blade. She reacted with the speed and agility that other fights had brought to her, reaching out and wrenching Lucian's neck her way, placing the younger man's body between her and the projectile now headed her way.

The blade thudded into Lucian's back.

His eyes went wide with fear and pain.

She released her grip and he dropped to the floor, not moving, blood pouring from the wound.

Travers immediately realized what had happened and switched the second knife from his left to right hand, readying another toss.

No way.

Not this time.

She shot him square in the chest.

Travers was thrown back, off his feet, and he slammed the tiled floor hard with the back of his head.

The knife clattered away.

She crossed the hall and kept the gun aimed.

Ready. Just in case.

He lay gripping his chest in pain, struggling to breathe. Blood seeped out from beneath the costume in steady rivulets. She stood over him, gun pointed down, and thought hard about what to do next.

Her old friend Henrik Thorvaldsen had told her once that when you crossed the threshold of good sense and morality and entered the realm of anger and revenge, it was truly *the end of forever*. Henrik's son had been brutally murdered, and he spent many years hunting for the killer. When he finally found him, the old Dane had consciously chosen to cross over the line. Sadly, Henrik was killed during the effort, and they'd never been able to discuss the journey. But she knew exactly what he would have told her. That they had discussed. More than once.

"*The law of retaliation is clear,*" he said. "*Lex talionis. A person who injures another is to be penalized to a similar degree by the injured party.*"

"*But that doesn't mean revenge,*" she'd told him. "*Vengeance plays no part in an eye for an eye. That part of the Talmud refers only to compensation for a wrong. Not violence for violence.*"

"*There is only one form of compensation for the loss of my son.*"

And the same was true for Esmerelda.

Just one.

She kept the gun aimed, finger on the trigger, watching Travers for a flicker of an eyelid. A tiny twitch at the corner of his mouth. A jerk of a hand. Anything to justify her pulling the trigger one more time. A drop of sweat slid in a slow track from her forehead to her chin.

Travers glared at her.

Defiant. Unrepentant.

This man had no conscious. No morals. No redeeming qualities at all.

But murder?

She thought of Esmerelda and all the joy that woman had brought to her life. All the good things she'd done for so many. And her two children. Truly, a wonderful human being.

Slaughtered.

For nothing.

Was this how Henrik had felt when he finally faced his son's killers in Paris? Empowered? Emboldened? Sure? Nothing standing in the way any longer for the satisfaction?

There truly was a sense of turning a corner, choosing a course that could never be reversed.

A moral line crossed.

The end of forever.

Henrik died, never having to live with his choice.

Could she?

Only one way to find out.

Travers' breath caught. He clutched at the wound to his chest, which continued to bleed. She stared down at him, watching, as the life left his eyes and he drew in the last bits of oxygen his lungs would ever need.

Then he lay still.

And silent.

Dead.

She lowered the gun.

And closed her eyes.

It was over.

Epilogue

CASSIOPEIA EXAMINED THE CASTLE CONSTRUCTION SITE.

Two weeks had passed since San Marino. Within a minute of Travers' dying the local police had arrived and she told them all that happened, aided by Anneke, who'd landed the chopper and made her way back up to the city. Eventually, the *Direction Générale de la Sécurité Extérieure* intervened with the Italian authorities and explained that it had been an ongoing French intelligence operation which Cassiopeia Vitt had aided in resolving. As she'd suspected, no one had shed a tear that Robert Travers was dead.

Good riddance had been the general sentiment.

The hard part came when she flew to Spain and explained to Jocasta and Pedro that their mother had been murdered because of something she'd done to Travers. All of it bit at her heart with a fury she'd never experienced before and hoped to never feel again. But they were understanding, not blaming her in any way, both saying that their mother had been involved with bringing down the Repository too. No way for any of them to know the degree of vengeance that Robert Travers would seek.

At least they had answers. The truth.

Now life had to go on.

Nicodème had been relieved when she finally made contact with him. She'd been missing from his shop for two days, and he'd alerted the authorities. The helicopter pilot, who'd been waiting for her outside of Eze, had also been concerned. But she'd escaped Travers' quandary herself before the authorities could make any headway.

Cotton had been supportive and appreciative. After all, she had saved his life. He'd come up to the museum with the authorities and had been shocked to see her. She'd told him about the choice she'd been contemplating and how fate intervened and ended Travers' life. He was glad that happened. He and Henrik Thorvaldsen had not been on good terms when Henrik died. To this day Cotton regretted that bitter parting. But he also regretted the choices their old friend had made. *You couldn't live with yourself if you'd pulled the trigger again,* he'd told her.

And he was right.

Would you have shot him a second time?, he'd asked her.

Good question. Would she have? The first time was clearly self-defense. The second would have something more entirely. God knows she'd wanted to. But, unlike with Henrik, the final decision had been taken away from her.

Thank goodness.

The construction site was returning to normal. The debris had been cleared and the quarrymen were fast extracting more stone and hewing new building blocks. Jean Claude had spent a couple of days in the hospital but was otherwise fine. Everyone was busy trying to get things back on track, and she appreciated their dedication and enthusiasm.

All of Travers' assets were immediately seized by the European Union, including his ship, bank accounts, and every other tangible item that could be located and confiscated. His arms dealing company had been shut down, its entire operation halted. It would take years to sort through things, but the Leprechaun was no more.

Cotton was back in Denmark, and she'd not heard from him today. A lot had happened over the past few weeks. Which seemed the story of her life.

Never a dull moment.

But she would not have it any other way. She hated with all her being that Esmerelda had paid the ultimate price. But she could not blame herself for what happened.

That was all on Travers.

At least Cotton and Nicodème were okay.

On her walk back from the construction site to her nearby chateau a text came in. WE NEVER MADE IT TO THE RIMINI RIVIERA FOR SWIMMING, EATING, AND OTHER THINGS. I CAN MEET YOU THERE TOMORROW.

She smiled.

And texted back.

I'LL SEE YOU THERE.

Writer's Note

Time now to separate fact from fiction.

The *erdstalls* described in chapters three and seven exist. They are a type of tunnel found throughout Europe, mainly in Bavaria and Austria, but also in France. Their origins and purposes are wholly unclear. Some say they were from the Dark Ages, others the Middle Ages, still others stretch them all the way back to the Stone Age. The word itself is from German, roughly meaning "earth stable" or "mining tunnel." *Erdstalls* are different from ordinary tunnels. Generally, they are low and narrow and oval shaped, aligned either vertically or horizontally. The most common length is between 70 to 170 feet. The *schlupf*, slip out, described in chapter seven is commonly part of their construction. These tight holes (usually around sixteen inches in diameter) served as transition points between tunnels of different elevations. The map depicted in chapter seven is of an actual *erdstall* site in Germany.

Why were they built? Nobody knows for sure. Folklore has linked them to legendary creatures, like elves or gnomes, who supposedly both built and lived in them. Others have speculated that they served as escape routes, but that interpretation ignores the fact that *erdstalls* have only one point of entry and exit. There is no back door. Others have suggested that the tunnels were hideouts, or perhaps storage bins. But their narrowness, coupled with a nearly zero air flow, would not make them well suited for either purpose. In addition, many of them lay below the local waterline and are prone to flooding.

The most bizarre claim is that they are part of some vast, interconnected network of subterranean passageways. An underground network dating to the Stone Age (which would make the tunnels 12,000 years old). Some sort of superhighway that allowed people to travel safely from one place to another, regardless of what was happening above them. As you might imagine there are countless problems with this fantasy, not the least of which is, while there are thousands of *erdstalls,* none are actually connected with each other.

The Republic of San Marino is the only surviving medieval microstate on the Italian peninsula. It spans a mere twenty-four square miles and is the oldest sovereign state and constitutional republic in the world. Supposedly, it is the fifth smallest country in the world. Mount

Titano sits at its heart, rising to 2,477 feet, and the City of San Marino (the capital) fills its slopes. The descriptions and locales from the city, mentioned throughout the story, are consistent with reality.

Its founding is fascinating.

The story goes that a man named Marinus, in the early part of the 4th century, left the island of Rab (in modern day Croatia) with his friend, Leo. Together, they made their way across the Adriatic Sea to Italy and the town of Rimini, where they established themselves as masons. Marinus preached Christian sermons there but was forced to flee during a period of Roman persecution, escaping to the nearby town of Monte Titano. There, in isolation, he built a church and established a mixed secularized and religious community that eventually led to the founding of the city-state San Marino. Marinus went on to be canonized as a saint, and his bones still rest in the Basilica di San Marino.

In 1631, the papacy formally recognized its independence. The inaccessible location and extreme poverty of its inhabitants made it a place conquerors avoided. In 1797 the French army finally threatened its independence, but because of the bravery and audacity of one of its captain regents, Napoleon spared it. When Italy unified in the 19th century, San Marino became a sanctuary for those opposed to the consolidation. During World War II it remained neutral, taking in around 100,000 refugees, eight times the population at that time. When Abraham Lincoln was offered a ceremonial citizenship, he praised San Marino as one of the *most honored countries in global history.*

Definitely worth a visit one day.

Also from M.J. Rose and Steve Berry

The House of Long Ago
A Cassiopeia Vitt Adventure

The time has come for Cassiopeia Vitt to sell her ancestral home. It sits on a Spanish bluff by the Mediterranean Sea, and bears the name *Casa de Hace Mucho Tiempo*, House of Long Ago. Trapped inside its walls are memories from a time when Cassiopeia was growing from a rebellious adolescent into a thoughtful young woman—regretful times when she often found herself estranged from her parents. Also inside are fifteen paintings, each one a masterpiece, together representing an investment in the tens of millions of euros—her father's private art collection—which she intends to donate to museums. But when an art expert declares all fifteen paintings fake, and suggests that her father may have been involved with something illegal, she embarks on a quest to find answers.

From a secret repository in Andorra, to a mysterious yacht in the Mediterranean, then finally onto the streets of Paris and a horrific reminder from World War II, Cassiopeia must battle every step of the way to stay alive—a fight that will finally bring her face to face with the truth about the House of Long Ago.

The Lake of Learning
A Cassiopeia Vitt Adventure

For over a decade Cassiopeia Vitt has been building an authentic French castle, using only materials and techniques from the 13th century. But when a treasure is unearthed at the construction site—an ancient Book of Hours—a multitude of questions are raised, all pointing to an ancient and forgotten religious sect.

Once the Cathars existed all across southern France, challenging Rome and attracting the faithful by the tens of thousands. Eventually, in 1208, the Pope declared them heretics and ordered a crusade—the first where Christians killed Christians—and thousands were slaughtered, the Cathars all but exterminated. Now a piece of that past has re-emerged, one that holds the key to the hiding place of the most precious object the Cathars possessed. And when more than one person becomes interested in that secret, in particular a thief and a billionaire, the race is on.

From the medieval walled city of Carcassonne, to the crest of mysterious Montségur, to a forgotten cavern beneath the Pyrenees, Cassiopeia is drawn deeper and deeper into a civil war between two people obsessed with revenge and murder.

The Museum of Mysteries
A Cassiopeia Vitt Adventure

Cassiopeia Vitt takes center stage in this exciting novella from New York Times bestsellers M.J. Rose and Steve Berry.

In the French mountain village of Eze, Cassiopeia visits an old friend who owns and operates the fabled Museum of Mysteries, a secretive place of the odd and arcane. When a robbery occurs at the museum, Cassiopeia gives chase to the thief and is plunged into a firestorm.

Through a mix of modern day intrigue and ancient alchemy, Cassiopeia is propelled back and forth through time, the inexplicable journeys leading her into a hotly contested French presidential election. Both candidates harbor secrets they would prefer to keep quiet, but an ancient potion could make that impossible. With intrigue that begins in southern France and ends in a chase across the streets of Paris, this magical, fast-paced, hold-your-breath thriller is all you've come to expect from M.J. Rose and Steve Berry.

The Kaiser's Web
A Cotton Malone Novel
By Steve Berry
Now Available

In *New York Times* bestseller Steve Berry's latest Cotton Malone adventure, a secret dossier from a World War II-era Soviet spy comes to light containing information that, if proven true, would not only rewrite history — it could impact Germany's upcoming national elections and forever alter the political landscape of Europe.

Two candidates are vying to become Chancellor of Germany. One is a patriot having served for the past sixteen years, the other a usurper, stoking the flames of nationalistic hate. Both harbor secrets, but only one knows the truth about the other. They are on a collision course, all turning on the events of one fateful day — April 30, 1945 — and what happened deep beneath Berlin in the Fürherbunker. Did Adolph Hitler and Eva Braun die there? Did Martin Bormann, Hitler's close confidant, manage to escape? And, even more important, where did billions in Nazi wealth disappear to in the waning days of World War II? The answers to these questions will determine not only who becomes the next Chancellor of Germany, but the fate of Europe as well.

From the mysterious Chilean lake district, to the dangerous mesas of South Africa, and finally into the secret vaults of Switzerland, former-Justice Department agent Cotton Malone discovers the truth about the fates of Hitler, Braun, and Bormann. Revelations that could not only transform Europe, but finally expose a mystery known as the Kaiser's web.

The Last Tiara
By M.J. Rose
Now Available

A provocative and moving story of a young female architect in post-World War II Manhattan who stumbles upon a hidden treasure and begins a journey to discovering her mother's life during the fall of the Romanovs.

Sophia Moon had always been reticent about her life in Russia and when she dies, suspiciously, on a wintry New York evening, Isobelle despairs that her mother's secrets have died with her. But while renovating the apartment they shared, Isobelle discovers something among her mother's effects — a stunning silver tiara, stripped of its jewels.

Isobelle's research into the tiara's provenance draws her closer to her mother's past — including the story of what became of her father back in Russia, a man she has never known. The facts elude her until she meets a young jeweler who wants to help her but is conflicted by his loyalty to the Midas Society, a covert international organization whose mission is to return lost and stolen antiques, jewels, and artwork to their original owners.

Told in alternating points of view, the stories of the two young women unfurl as each struggles to find their way during two separate wars. In 1915, young Sofiya Petrovitch, favorite of the royal household and best friend of Grand Duchess Olga Nikolaevna, tends to wounded soldiers in a makeshift hospital within the grounds of the Winter Palace in St. Petersburg and finds the love of her life. In 1948 New York, Isobelle Moon works to break through the rampant sexism of the age as one of very few women working in a male-dominated profession and discovers far more about love and family than she ever hoped for.

In the two narratives, the secrets of Sofiya's early life are revealed incrementally, even as Isobelle herself works to solve the mystery of the historic Romanov tiara (which is based on an actual Romanov artifact that is, to this day, still missing) and how it is that her mother came to possess it. The two strands play off each other in finely-tuned counterpoint, building to a series of surprising and deeply satisfying revelations.

The Steal

By C. W. Gortner and M.J. Rose
Coming August 10, 2021

They say diamonds are a girl's best friend—until they're stolen.

Ania Throne is devoted to her jewelry company. The daughter of one of the world's most famous jewelers, she arrives in Cannes with a stunning new collection. But a shocking theft by the notorious thief known as the Leopard throws her into upheaval—and plunges her on an unexpected hunt that challenges everything she believes.

Jerome Curtis thinks he's seen it all, especially when it comes to crime. Until he's hired to investigate the loss of Ania Thorne's collection, his every skill put to the test as he chases after a mysterious master-mind responsible for some of the costliest heists in history—and finds himself in a tangled web with a woman he really shouldn't fall in love with.

From the fabled Carlton Hotel to the elegant boulevards of Paris, Ania and Jerome must race against time to catch a thief before the thief catches them. With everything on the line, can they solve the steal or will the steal take more than diamonds from them?

Set in the late 1950s, THE STEAL is a romantic caper by bestselling authors C.W. Gortner and M.J. Rose.

About Steve Berry

STEVE BERRY is the New York Times and #1 internationally bestselling author of sixteen Cotton Malone novels and four standalones. He has 25 million books in print, translated into 41 languages. With his wife, Elizabeth, he is the founder of History Matters, which is dedicated to historical preservation. He serves as an emeritus member on the Smithsonian Libraries Advisory Board and was a founding member of International Thriller Writers, formerly serving as its co-president.

About M.J. Rose

New York Times bestseller M.J. Rose grew up in New York City mostly in the labyrinthine galleries of the Metropolitan Museum, the dark tunnels and lush gardens of Central Park and reading her mother's favorite books before she was allowed. She believes mystery and magic are all around us but we are too often too busy to notice... books that exaggerate mystery and magic draw attention to it and remind us to look for it and revel in it.

Please visit her blog, Museum of Mysteries at http://www.mjrose.com/blog/

Rose's work has appeared in many magazines including *Oprah* magazine and she has been featured in the *New York Times, Newsweek, Wall Street Journal, Time, USA Today* and on the Today Show, and NPR radio. Rose graduated from Syracuse University, spent the '80s in advertising, has a commercial in the Museum of Modern Art in New York City and since 2005 has run the first marketing company for authors - Authorbuzz.com.

Rose lives in Connecticut with her husband, the musician and composer Doug Scofield.